MISUNDERSTOOD

Title: Misunderstood

Author: Florence Montgomery

Release Date: July 29, 2017 [EBook #55222]

Language: English

*** START OF THIS PROJECT GUTENBERG EBOOK
MISUNDERSTOOD ***

MISUNDERSTOOD

BY

FLORENCE MONTGOMERY,

AUTHOR OF

**"A VERY SIMPLE STORY," and "PEGGY AND OTHER TALES,"
"THROWN TOGETHER."**

**NEW YORK:
ANSON D. F. RANDOLPH & COMPANY,
38 WEST TWENTY-THIRD STREET.**

NEW YORK:

EDWARD O. JENKINS,   ROBERT RUTTER,
Printer and Stereotyper,   *Binder*,
20 North William St.   116 and 118 East 14th Street.

TO

THE HON. MRS. AUGUSTUS LIDDELL

THE FOLLOWING STORY

IS

Dedicated.

CONTENTS

	PAGE
PREFACE.	5 ....
	7 ....
	7 ....
	31 .....
	62 .....
	76 .....
	100 ...
	109 ...
	141 ...
	150 ...
	159 ...
	178 ...
	187 ...
	201 ...
	213 ...

215 ...
225 ...
240 ...
257 ...
279 ...

PART I.
CHAPTER I.
CHAPTER II.
CHAPTER III.
CHAPTER IV.
CHAPTER V.
CHAPTER VI.
CHAPTER VII.
CHAPTER VIII.
CHAPTER IX.
CHAPTER X.
CHAPTER XI.
CHAPTER XII.
PART II.
CHAPTER XIII.
CHAPTER XIV.
CHAPTER XV.
CHAPTER XVI.
CHAPTER XVII.

PREFACE.

The following is not a child's story. It is intended for those who are interested in children; for those who are willing to stoop to view life as it appears to a child, and to enter for half-an-hour into the manifold small interests, hopes, joys, and trials which make up its sum.

It has been thought that the lives of children, as known by themselves, from their own little point of view, are not always sufficiently realized; that they are sometimes overlooked or misunderstood; and to throw some light, however faint, upon the subject, is one of the objects of this little story.

So much of it has been gathered from observation and recollection, that the author cannot help hoping it may not entirely fail of its aim.

MISUNDERSTOOD.

In Two Parts.

PART I.

CHAPTER I.

Ever since the nursery dinner has the rain come pouring down all over the fields and meadows, the lawns and gardens, the roofs and gables of old Wareham Abbey, in the county of Sussex.

Ever since the cloth was cleared away have two little curly heads been pressed close together at the nursery window, and two pair of eager eyes been watching the clouds and sky.

What a dreadful wet afternoon! It is so particularly tiresome, as their father is expected home to-day, and had promised the two little brothers that they should come and meet him at the station.

There would be no room for Virginie in the dog-cart, and so, if they promised to sit very still, and not stand on the wheel to get in, or jump out before the carriage had stopped, or do anything else equally extraordinary, they were to have been trusted to old Peter, the coachman, and what fun *that* would have been!

To get away from Virginie for so long was the height of human enjoyment. She seemed to them a being created on purpose to interfere with every plan of enjoyment, to foresee danger where they only saw fun, and so bring the shadow of her everlasting "Ne faites pas ceci, ne faites pas cela," across the sunny path of their boyish schemes and pastimes.

Poor Virginie! if she had been brought to the bar of their young judgments, she would have been at once condemned without any reference to extenuating circumstances. And yet she was, in the main a good, well-meaning woman, but unfortunately gifted with "nerves;" and the responsibility of the entire charge of the children of a widower, who was a great deal away from home, made her life an anxious one, more especially as they were a pair of the most reckless creatures that ever were born—fearless of danger, heedless of consequences, and deaf to entreaty or remonstrance.

Little Miles, the youngest, as she often told their father, was well enough *alone*; she could manage him perfectly, for, being only four years old, he was amenable to authority; but "Monsieur Humphrey!"

Words always failed Virginie at this juncture. She could only throw up her hands, and raise her eyes to the ceiling, with a suppressed exclamation.

Sir Everard Duncombe was a member of Parliament, and during the session was almost entirely in London, so that beyond his Saturday to Monday at the Abbey, his children saw but little of him at this time of the year.

During these flying visits he was overwhelmed with complaints of all M. Humphrey had done during the past week: how he would climb impossible trees and jump from impossible heights; how he had gone into the stables right under the horses' heels, or taken a seat in the kennel, with the blood-hound; how narrowly he had escaped tumbling over the ha-ha one day, and slipping into the pond the next; in fact there was no end to his misdemeanors.

But the point on which Virginie harped was, that he led his little brother into all sorts of mischief; for what Humphrey did, Miles would do too, and where Humphrey went, Miles was ready to follow.

It was quite another thing, as Virginie urged, for Miles. Humphrey was proof against colds, coughs, and accidents of all kinds; but little Miles was physically weaker, and had moreover a tendency to a delicate chest and to croup; so that cold winds, and wet feet, and over-exertion, could not be too carefully avoided.

Timid and gentle by nature, clinging and affectionate by disposition, he was just the child a father delights in, and to him Sir Everard's affections were almost wholly given.

Lady Duncombe had observed her husband's partiality for his younger boy for some time before her death, and had more than once taxed him with it.

"Miles is such a little coaxing thing," he answered, taking the child up in his arms, and stroking the little curly head which

4

nestled at once so contentedly down on his shoulder. "If I took Humphrey up, he would struggle to get down, and be climbing over the tables and chairs."

"Humphrey is three years older," argued Lady Duncombe; "you could not expect him to sit so still as a baby not yet two: but he is quite as affectionate as Miles, in a different way."

"It may be so," Sir Everard returned "but it is very engaging when a little creature clings to one in this way, and sits for hours in one's lap."

Lady Duncombe did not answer, but her eye wandered from the fair-haired baby and rested on her eldest boy, who for three years had been her only child. To her, at least, he was an object of pride and pleasure. She gloried in his manly ways, his untiring spirits and activity; and loved his rough caresses quite as well as the more coaxing ways of his baby brother.

How she delighted to see him come rushing headlong into the room, and make one bound into her lap, even if he *did* knock down a chair or so on his way, upset her work-box and its contents, and dirty the sofa with his muddy boots. What then! Did not his eager kisses rain upon her cheek? Were not his dear rough arms round her neck? Did she not *know* what a loving heart beat under his apparent heedlessness and forgetfulness? What if he forgot every injunction and every promise, if he did not forget *her*! What if he took heed of no one and nothing, if her look and her kiss were always sought and cared for!

Oh! it was a sad day for little Humphrey Duncombe when that mother was taken away from him: when the long, wasting illness ended in death: when the hollow eye, which to the last had rested on him, closed for ever on this world; and the thin, transparent hands were folded for the last time on the breast where he should never again hide his curly head, and sob out his confessions and repentance.

Sir Everard, overwhelmed by the blow which had fallen on him, hardly saw his children during the early days of his bereavement.

When he did, he was surprised to find Humphrey much the same as ever; still noisy and heedless, still full of mischief, and apparently forgetful of what had happened.

"He has not much heart," was his inward comment, as he watched the little figure, in its deep mourning, chasing the young lambs in the meadow.

Sir Everard saw the boy to all appearance the same, because he saw him in his moments of forgetfulness, when nature and childhood had asserted their rights, and the buoyancy of the boy's disposition had enabled him to throw off the memory of his sorrow: but he did *not* see him when the sense of his loss was upon him; did not see the face change, when the recollection came over him; did not hear the familiar name half uttered, and then choked by a sob. He did not see the rush to the drawing-room, with some new treasure, some new plan to be unfolded—and the sudden stop at the door, as the thought swept over him that on the well-known sofa there is now no mother's smile awaiting him, no ever-ready ear to listen and sympathize, no loving kiss, no responsive voice: and the low sob of pain, the listless drop of the arms to the side, and the rush away into the open air, away and away, anywhere, to escape from the grief and the longing, and the blank sense of desolation.

Only He, who dwelling in the highest heaven, yet vouchsafes to behold the lowest creature here upon earth, knew what was in the heart of the boy; as no one but He saw the pillow wet with tears, and heard the cry breaking forth in the dead of the night from the inmost recesses of the poor little orphaned heart. "Oh, mother! mother! what shall I do without you!"

All this had happened nearly two years before the day of which I am speaking, when the rain was acting its time-hackneyed part before the two little spectators at the window.

It had faded out of little Miles' mind as if it had never been; he could not even remember his mother; but in the mind of the elder boy her memory was still, at times, fresh and green.

Weeks and months might pass without his thoughts dwelling on her, but all of a sudden, a flower, a book, or some little thing that had belonged to her, would bring it all back, and then the little chest would heave, the curly head would droop, and the merry brown eyes be dimmed by a rush of tears.

There was a full-length picture in the now unused drawing-room of Lady Duncombe, with Humphrey in her arms; and at these times, or when he was in some trouble with Virginie, the boy would steal in there, and lie curled up on the floor in the darkened room; putting himself in the same attitude that he was in in the picture, and then try to fancy he felt her arms round him, and her shoulder against his head.

There were certain days when the room was scrubbed and dusted; when the heavy shutters were opened, and the daylight streamed upon the picture. Then the two little brothers might be seen standing before it, while the elder detailed to the younger all he could remember about her.

Miles had the greatest respect and admiration for Humphrey. A boy of seven, who wears knickerbockers, is always an object of veneration to one of four, who is as yet limited to blouses: but Miles' imagination could not soar beyond the library and dining-room; and he could not remember the drawing-room otherwise than a closed room; so his respect grew and intensified as he listened to Humphrey's glowing description of the past glories of the house, when the drawing-room was one blaze of light, when there were muslin curtains in the windows, and chintz on all the chairs; and mother lay on the sofa, with her work-table by her side.

Dim and shadowy was the little fellow's idea of the "mother" of whom his brother always spoke in softened tones and with glistening eyes; but that she was something very fair and holy he was quite sure.

Deep was his sense of his inferiority to Humphrey in this respect; and a feeling akin to shame would steal over him when one of their long conversations would be abruptly put an end to by

Humphrey's quick, contemptuous "It's no use trying to make you understand, because you don't remember her."

A very wistful look would come over the pretty little face on these occasions, and he would humbly admit his great degradation.

It was Miles' admiration for his brother that was the bane of Virginie's life. Timid by nature, Miles became bold when Humphrey led the way; obedient and submissive by himself, at Humphrey's bidding he would set Virginie at defiance, and for the time be as mischievous as he.

That "l'union fait la force," Virginie had long since discovered, to the ruin of her nerves and temper.

And now Virginie has several times suggested that if Humphrey will submit to a water-proof coat, and goloshes, he may go and meet his father at the station; and Humphrey has consented to come to terms if Miles may go too.

But here Virginie is firm. No amount of wrapping up would prevent Miles catching cold on so damp and rainy a day, as she knows well, by fatal experience; so the fiat has gone forth, either Humphrey will go alone, or both will stay at home.

"Don't go," pleaded little Miles, as they pressed their faces against the window; "it will be so dull all alone with Virginie."

"She's a cross old thing," muttered Humphrey; "but never mind, Miles, I won't go without you, and we'll count the raindrops on the window to make the time pass quick."

This interesting employment had the desired effect, and the next half-hour soon slipped by. Indeed, it was so engrossing, that the dog-cart came up the avenue, and was nearly at the hall door, before the little boys perceived it.

"Qu'est-ce que c'est donc!" exclaimed Virginie, startled by Humphrey's jump from the window-sill to the floor.

"C'est mon père," was all the information he vouchsafed her, as he rushed out of the room.

"M. votre père! Attendez done que je vous arrange un peu les cheveux."

She spoke to the winds: nothing was heard of Humphrey but sundry bumps and jumps in the distance, which told of his rapid descent down the stairs.

The more tardy Miles was caught and brushed, in spite of his struggles, and then he was off to join his brother.

He reached the hall door just as the carriage drove up, and the two little figures jumped and capered about, while a tall, dark gentleman divested himself of his mackintosh and umbrella, and then came up the steps into the house.

He stooped down to kiss the eager faces. "Well, my little fellows, and how are you both? No bones broken since last week? No new bruises and bumps, eh?"

They were so taken up with their father, that they did not perceive that he was not alone, but that another gentleman had got out of the dog-cart, till Sir Everard said—

"Now go and shake hands with that gentleman. I wonder if you know who he is?"

Humphrey looked up into the young man's face, and said, while his color deepened—

"I think you are my Uncle Charlie, who came to see us once a long time ago before you went to sea, and before——"

"Quite right," said Sir Everard, shortly; "I did not think you would have remembered him. I daresay, Charlie, Humphrey has not altered very much; but this little fellow was quite a baby when you went away," he added, taking Miles up in his arms, and looking at his brother-in-law for admiration.

"What a likeness!" exclaimed Uncle Charlie.

Sir Everard put the child down with a sigh.

"Like in more ways than one, I am afraid. Look here," pointing to the delicate tracery of the blue veins on the forehead, and the flush on the fair cheek.

Humphrey had been listening intently to this conversation, and his father being once more occupied with kissing Miles, he advanced to his uncle, and put his hand confidingly in his.

"You are a nice little man," said Uncle Charlie, laying his other hand on the curly head; "we were always good friends, Humphrey. But," he added, half to himself, as he turned up the bright face to his, and gazed at it intently for a moment, "you are not a bit like your mother."

The dressing-gong now sounded, and the little boys proceeded to their father's room, to help or hinder him with his toilette.

Miles devoted himself to the carpet-bag, in expectation of some tempting paper parcel; while Humphrey's attentions were given to first one and then the other of the articles he was extracting from the pocket of the coat Sir Everard had just thrown off.

A suspicious click made the baronet turn round.

"What have you got hold of, Humphrey?"

An open pocket-knife dropped from the boy's hand he had just succeeded in opening the two blades, and was in the act of trying the edges on his thumb nail.

Failing in that experiment, his restless fingers strayed to the dressing-table, and an ominous silence ensued.

"Humphrey," shouted his father, "put my razor down."

In the glass he had caught sight of a well-soaped face, and spoke just in time to stop the operation.

Punishment always follows sin, and Humphrey was dispatched to the nursery to have his face sponged and dried.

By taking a slide down the banisters, however, he made up for lost time, and arrived at the library-door at the same time as his father and brother.

Uncle Charlie was standing by the window, ready dressed; and the gong sounding at that moment, they all went in to dinner.

The two little brothers had a chair on each side of their father, and an occasional share in his food.

Dinner proceeded in silence. Uncle Charlie was enjoying his soup, and Sir Everard, dividing himself between his little boys and his meal.

"It's William's birthday to-day," said Humphrey, breaking silence.

The unfortunate individual in white silk stockings, thus suddenly brought into public notice, reddened to the roots of his hair; and in his confusion nearly dropped the dish he was in the act of putting down before his master.

"He's twenty-two years old to-day," continued Humphrey; "he told me so this morning."

Sir Everard tried to evince a proper amount of interest in so important an announcement.

"What o'clock were you born, William?" pursued Humphrey, addressing the shy young footman at the side-board, where he had retreated with the dish-cover, and from whence he was making all sorts of signs to his tormentor, in the vain hope of putting an end to the conversation.

Sir Everard hastily held out a bit of turbot on the end of his fork, and effectually stopped the boy's mouth for a few minutes; but no sooner had he swallowed it, than he broke out again.

"What are you going to give William for his birthday present, father?" he said, putting his arms on the table, and resting his chin upon them, that he might the more conveniently look up into his father's face, and await his answer.

Lower and lower bent Uncle Charlie's head over his plate, and his face became alarmingly suffused with color.

"I know what he'd like," finished Humphrey, "for he's told me!"

The unhappy footman snatched up a dish-cover, and began a retreat to the door; but the inexorable butler handed him the lobster sauce, and he was obliged to advance with it to his master's side.

"I said to him to-day," proceeded Humphrey, in all the conscious glory of being in William's confidence, "If father were to give you a birthday present, what would you like? You remember, don't you, William? And then he told me, didn't you, William?"

The direct form of attack was more than flesh and blood could stand. William made a rush to the door with the half-filled tray and, in spite of furious glances from the butler, disappeared, just as Uncle Charlie gave it up as a bad job, and burst out laughing.

"You must not talk quite so much at dinner, my boy," said Sir Everard, when the door was shut; "your uncle and I have not been able to say a word. I assure you," he added in an under tone to his brother-in-law, "these children keep me in constant hot water; I never know what they will say next."

When the servants reappeared the gentlemen, to William's relief, were talking politics; and Humphrey was devoting his energies to digging graves in the salt, and burying therein imaginary corpses, represented by pills he was forming from his father's bread.

"Will you come and help me with my dinner, next week, Charlie?" said Sir Everard; "I am going to entertain the aborigines, and I shall want a little assistance. It is now more than two years since I paid my constituents any attention, and I feel the time has come."

"What long words," said Humphrey, *sotto voce*, as he patted down the last salt grave, and stuck a bit of parsley, that had dropped from the fish, on the top of the mound. "Father," he went on, "what are abo—abo—"

"Aborigines?" finished Uncle Charlie. "Wild men of the woods, Humphrey; half human beings, half animals."

"And is father going to have them to dinner?" exclaimed Humphrey, in great astonishment.

"Yes," said Uncle Charlie, enjoying the joke; "it will be fine fun for you and Miles, won't it?"

"Oh, won't it!" echoed Humphrey, jumping down from his chair, and capering about. "Oh, father! will you promise, before you even ask Virginie, that we may come down to dinner that night, and see them?"

"Well, I don't know about dinner," said Sir Everard; "little boys are rather in the way on these occasions, especially those who don't know how to hold their tongues when they ought; but you shall both come down in the library and see them arrive."

At this moment Virginie's unwelcome head appeared at the door, and her unwelcome voice proclaimed, "M. Humphrey, M. Miles, il faut venir vous coucher."

Very unwillingly did they obey, for the conversation had reached a most interesting point, and Humphrey had a hundred and one questions still to put about the aborigines.

They proceeded quietly upstairs, closely followed by Virginie, who always liked to see them well on in front of her, in case they should take it into their heads to do anything very extraordinary on their way.

To-night, however, they were much too full of the wild men of the woods they were to see on Friday to think of anything else, and they arrived in the bed-room nursery, without giving any shocks to Virginie's nervous system.

Indeed, the subject lasted them till they were undressed, and washed, and tucked up in their little beds side by side.

Virginie shut the shutters, and with a sigh of relief retired to supper.

"I'm glad she's gone," said Humphrey, "because now we can have a good talk about the wild men."

"Oh, Humphie!" said little Miles beseechingly, "*please* don't let us talk of them any more now it's dark; or if you really *must*, give me your hand to hold, for it does frighten me so."

"Then we won't talk about them," said the elder boy in a soothing tone, as he drew close to the edge of the bed, and threw his arm protectingly round the little one. Miles nestled close up to him, and with their cheeks one against the other, and hands tightly clasped together, they fell asleep.

Poor little curly heads, o'er whom no fond mother shall bend to-night, murmuring soft words of love and blessing! Poor dimpled faces, on whom no lingering kiss shall fall!

Outside in the meadows, the young lambs lay by the ewe's side; up in the trees the wee birds nestled beneath the parent wing, but no light step, no softly rustling gown, no carefully shaded light, disturbed the dreamless slumber of the two little brothers.

CHAPTER II.

Sir Everard Duncombe did not make his appearance in the dining-room till nine o'clock, but long before that hour his movements were known to the whole household; for soon after eight, the two little boys were stationed outside his door, and failing to gain admittance, kept account of the progress of his toilette, in tones which were heard all over the house.

"Will you soon be out of your bath, father?... Are you just about soaping?... What are you doing now?... Are you sponging now?... What a splash father is having! He must be drying himself now, he is so very quiet."

Then sounded the unlocking of a door, and the scamper of little feet.

"I must congratulate you on the satisfactory way in which you performed your ablutions this morning," was Uncle Charlie's salutation to his brother-in-law, as he entered the breakfast room with a boy on each side of him.

Sir Everard laughed. "There are no secrets in this house, you see," he answered, as he shook hands. "What a lovely day!"

"Glorious! but it is going to be very hot. If I remember right, the walk to church is shady all the way. Do these little fellows go to church?"

"Not Miles, but I generally take Humphrey; and wonderful to say he is as quiet as possible. I really think church is the only place in the world where he can sit still."

Humphrey was engaged during the whole of breakfast time in finding the places in his prayer-book, and was too much occupied to talk.

"There!" he exclaimed triumphantly, as he put in the last marker, and restrained himself with a violent effort as he was about to throw his prayer-book in the air, "now they are all found."

15

"And now you had better go and dress," said his father, "so as not to keep your uncle and me waiting."

Humphrey joined them in the hall at the last minute, having been detained by a skirmish with Virginie.

Their way to church lay through the flower-garden and down the avenue. They went out by the side-door, leaving Miles looking disconsolately after them, his pretty little face and slight figure framed in the old doorway.

They walked on together in silence for some time.

Sir Everard was enjoying the calm beauty of the summer day; Humphrey was in pursuit of a butterfly; and Uncle Charlie was looking round at the evidences of his dead sister's taste in the laying out of the flower-garden, and thinking of the last time he had walked through it to church, when she had been by his side.

"How hot that boy will make himself before we get to church," said Sir Everard, presently; "I really don't know what he is made of, to run on a day like this."

"He is a fine boy," said Uncle Charlie, as he watched the active little figure skipping over the flower-beds, "and seems as strong and well as possible."

"Yes," said the baronet, "Humphrey has never had a day's illness in his life. He takes after my family, and is going to be as strong and as tall as they."

"He is very like some of the old family pictures I was looking at this morning; the same upright, well-built figure, and dark eyes. Now Miles is altogether different, so fair and slender."

"I fear Miles inherits his mother's constitution," answered the baronet, in a troubled tone. "He is very delicate, Charlie, and the least chill brings on croup, or a nasty little cough. I feel very anxious about him sometimes."

"I daresay he will grow out of it. I believe I had a delicate chest at his age, and I am never troubled with it now."

They were some way down the avenue, and Humphrey was nowhere to be seen.

"I never wait for him," said Sir Everard, as he opened the park gates; "he always turns up at last."

They were half-way across the churchyard when the boy overtook them, flushed and breathless.

Uncle Charlie inwardly groaned at the thoughts of so restless a mortal, as a next-door neighbor, during two hours' service on a hot summer's morning, and watched his movements with some anxiety.

Little Humphrey took off his hat in the porch, shook back his curly hair from his hot forehead, and walked quietly into church.

He led the way to the chancel, where was the old fashioned family pew.

Here he came to a dead stop, for the bolt of the door was high above his reach.

His uncle undid it for him, and was about to pass in, thinking that of course the child would sit by his father; but to his surprise, his little nephew pushed past him, went to the very end of the long pew, and clambered up the high-cushioned seat opposite a big prayer-book, which was surmounted with the monogram "Adelaide."

The rustic congregation had often wondered why the father and son sat at so great a distance from each other in the pew that so seldom had any occupants but themselves; and the old clergyman had at first with difficulty suppressed a smile at the view from the pulpit, of the broad shoulders and bearded face of the six foot man at one extremity, and the top of the small brown head at the other.

But in vain had Sir Everard invited the boy to sit nearer to him; he preferred his isolation. It had once occurred to the widower that it might be because it had been his wife's place; but he never gave Humphrey credit for much heart or sentiment, so he had settled it was a mere whim and never asked the boy any questions on the subject.

The child himself had never confided to anyone but Miles how he loved to feel he was looking at the very same bit of the painted window which his mother's eyes had fallen upon; that his feet were on the very same footstool that her's had rested on; and though the big prayer-book was too heavy for him to open, he liked to put his own little morocco volume upon it, and to press his little fingers on the "Adelaide" that formed the monogram of her name.

He could not have explained what there was about the old church that brought back to him more than anything else the memory of his mother, but so it was: and the usually restless boy would sit quiet in his corner, and think of the first Sunday he had come to church, when he had read out of the same prayer-book with her, and listened to her sweet voice as she joined in the Psalms and Hymns.

The service began, and Humphrey struggled down from his seat.

The villagers had grown accustomed, when the congregation stood up, to see the baronet rise tall and broad from his seat, and the little brown head of his son disappear altogether; but Uncle Charlie was by no means prepared for so complete a collapse, and thought his nephew had fallen. However, there he was, standing on the ground, with his eyes fixed on his prayer-book, and the walls of the pew towering over him on every side.

"Why on earth does he not stand on a stool?" was the young man's inward reflection.

Truth to say, the temptation to gain three feet in height, and get a view of what was passing around, *had* at times assailed Humphrey, but he felt sure his mother had never stood on the stool, and so he resisted the inclination.

And, indeed, if Lady Duncombe had mounted the very high structure which went by the name of a hassock, the effect would have been a trial to the gravity of the congregation.

Humphrey followed the service pretty well till the chanting began, and here he always got wrong. Do what he would he could not keep time with the rest, but always arrived at the end of the verse either too early or too late.

By slow degrees he had discovered that it did not do to sing straight through to the end, because there were some bits and words they sang over again; but *how* he was ever to discover which particular word or sentence they were going to repeat, was to him a perpetual puzzle.

He had a great admiration for the turns and shakes with which the old clerk varied the "Te Deum," and had once indulged in a mild imitation of the same; till he caught sight of his father frowning at him from the other end of the pew.

When the hymn was given out, Uncle Charlie saw Humphrey in great difficulties over finding his place, so he made a sign to him to come and share *his* hymn-book; but, with a most decided shake of the head, Humphrey produced his own, and, without moving from his place, held it out to have his place found.

As the young man returned it to his nephew, he saw on the fly-leaf the name "Adelaide Duncombe," in the well-known handwriting of his dead sister; and he did justice to the boy's motive.

When the old clergyman opened his sermon-book, Humphrey settled himself in his corner, in exact imitation of his father.

It always took him some time to copy the position, and sometimes, when he had just accomplished it, Sir Everard would uncross his leg, or move a hand, and then he was quite discomfited, and had to begin all over again.

To-day, however, his attitude was quite simple. Sir Everard folded his arms, crossed his legs, and turning his head to the pulpit, disposed himself to listen.

Humphrey did the same.

Then rose the voice of the old clergyman "In the fourteenth chapter of the Book of the Revelation of St. John, and at the second verse, you will find the word of God thus written: 'And I heard a voice from heaven, as the voice of many waters, ... and I heard the harpers harping with their harps.... And they sang as it were a new song, and no man could learn that song but the hundred and forty and four thousand, which were redeemed from the earth.'" ...

Humphrey did not often listen to the sermon, but to-day it was all about Heaven, and he liked to hear about that, because his mother was there.

Feeble must human language ever be to paint the glories of that far-off land; but when men touch upon subjects that so vitally concern all, they carry their hearers with them.

And so it was, that as the old preacher warmed and glowed with his theme, the hearts of the congregation warmed and glowed too; and there was silence and deep attention in the old church that day.

Even the village school children fidgeted less than usual, and one or two smock-frocks who had settled themselves in their usual attitude, of arms crossed on the back of the bench in front of them, and heads cradled thereupon, shook off the drowsiness consequent on their long, hot walk to church, and sitting up, gave their attention to the sermon. For were not one and all bound to the land the preacher was describing? And was there one who could say, "What is this to me?"

Only twice was even Humphrey's attention distracted. The first time was when he saw his uncle take a pencil out of his pocket, and underline something in his Bible. This was altogether a novel proceeding; Humphrey had never seen it done before, and he felt it incumbent upon him to sidle along the pew-seat up to his uncle to investigate the matter.

Uncle Charlie gave him his Bible, and he saw that the text of the sermon was the passage marked.

He inwardly resolved, as he regained his corner by the shuffling process before mentioned, that *he* would in future bring a pencil to church and do likewise.

The next disturbance was of a more exciting character. A vagrant wasp, after disporting itself in different parts of the church, made an inroad into the family pew, and fixed upon Uncle Charlie as its victim. Humphrey, attracted by the buzzing, turned round, and saw his uncle engaged in desperate conflict.

Bobbing his head first to one side, and then to the other, now drawing himself suddenly back, and now as suddenly swerving forward, every now and then making a frantic grab in the air with the back of his hand, Uncle Charlie strove to escape from his assailant in vain.

Humphrey tried hard to keep his countenance as he watched the encounter, but it would not do. The merry smile broke out from every corner of his face, and, in great alarm, he crammed his hands into his mouth to stifle the laughter he felt would, in another moment, break out.

Uncle Charlie was already very angry at being disqualified from listening to a sermon he was enjoying by so paltry a cause as the attacks of a wasp, and now, when he saw his nephew's condition, he grew desperate.

Seizing a hymn-book, he made a plunge at his tormentor, and brought it to the ground, where he crushed it to atoms with his heel; and with a sensation of great relief saw Humphrey's countenance return to an expression of becoming composure, and found himself in a condition to take up the thread of the discourse.

Humphrey's attention was once more riveted on the sermon, and his little mind strove to follow the clergyman as he spoke of the white-robed thousands wandering by the jasper sea in the golden Jerusalem; that "great multitude which no man can number of all kindreds, and nations, and tongues;" uniting their songs in the same burst of glorious psalmody as the "voice of many waters," and as the voice of mighty thunderings, saying, "Alleluia; for the Lord God omnipotent reigneth."

"'Eye hath not seen,'" concluded the preacher, as if in despair of finding words to express the inconceivable glory and beauty of the halls of Sion, "'eye hath not seen, nor ear heard, neither hath it entered into the heart of man the things which God hath prepared for them that love Him.' To Him, who bought them for us with his own blood, be glory for ever, and to countless ages."

Then the organ broke forth, doors opened and shut, the school-boys clattered down from the organ loft, and the congregation streamed out of church; leaving the old clergyman standing in his pulpit, gazing thoughtfully at the retreating throng, and wondering how much of what he had endeavored to impress upon their hearts would take root downwards, and bear fruit upwards.

Sir Everard Duncombe remained sitting some time after the service was over, looking at Humphrey's earnest face, and wondering what the boy was thinking of. When the clergyman had retired to the vestry, he rose, and led the way out.

Softly blew the summer breezes on little Humphrey's face as he stepped out into the porch, and the calm beauty of the summer morning was in perfect harmony with the turn which the sermon had given to his thoughts. All around was the beautifully-wooded country, lying calm and still under the cloudless sky. Perhaps if his vague ideas could have taken shape, they would have formed themselves into some such expression as—"Can heaven be fairer than this?"

But Humphrey's was not a nature that could long remain absorbed in thought, and he was soon skipping along the road in front of his father and uncle, and kicking up clouds of dust with his best Sunday boots.

At the park gates they found Miles and Virginie. The latter joined the other servants in the road, and the two little brothers walked on together.

"Did the clergyman take any of my texts to-day for his sermon?" asked the younger one eagerly, as he took hold of Humphrey's hand. (Miles was learning the beatitudes, and asked the question regularly every Sunday.)

"No, not one of them. He got a text out of the very last bit of the whole Bible—'The Revelation.'"

"That must be the bit Virginie never will read to me. She says I should not understand it. Do you understand the Revelations, Humphie?"

"Yes," returned Humphrey, promptly.

"Virginie doesn't," said Miles rather puzzled, "and she says very few grown-up people do."

"Virginie is French," retorted Humphrey, "and the Revelations are written in English. Of course she can't understand them as well as I do. There goes a rabbit. Let's run after it."

And Miles, perfectly satisfied with the explanation, followed his brother, panting into the fern.

In the afternoon the gentlemen went again to church, and as Virginie was at liberty to do the same, the children were left under the care of the housemaid.

Humphrey was learning a hymn, and, for once in his life, giving his whole attention to his task.

Miles, sitting on the housemaid's lap, was turning over the leaves of the "Peep of Day," and gleaning his ideas of sacred characters from the illustrations of that well-known work. He stopped in great amazement before the representation of Lazarus rising from the tomb, and demanded an explanation.

Jane, who had an idea that everything connected with death should be most carefully concealed from children, answered evasively that it was nothing, and tried to turn over the page, but boys are not so easily baulked.

Had Miles been a girl, he would probably have been satisfied to pass over the picture without further inquiry; girls' minds take a very superficial grasp of a subject; they are content to get at the shell of knowledge, and to leave the kernel untasted. Being a boy,

Miles raised his large, grave eyes to Jane's face with an inquiring expression.

"Why don't you tell me?" he asked, laying a detaining hand on the leaf; "I want to know all about it. What is that great hole? and why is the man all sewed up in white?"

Jane, driven into a corner, admitted that the hole was a grave.

"But, lor! master Miles," added she, "you don't know nothing about them things, and if you want to know you must ask your pa!"

"Of course I know people die," said Miles, simply, "because my mamma's dead; so you're quite wrong, Jane, to say I don't understand those sort of things. I know all about it. When people die they are packed up in a box and put into the ground, and then if they've been good, God will come some day and unpack them."

Humphrey had joined the group just in time to hear the end of the explanation, and he met Jane's eye and smile with all the conscious superiority of his three years advance in religious knowledge.

"If mother were here, Miles," he whispered, "she would explain to you much better than that. There was something she used to tell me about our dead body being like a seed, that is, put into the ground, but will turn into a beautiful flower some day. Only I can't remember it quite like she said it," he added, sighing, "I wish I could."

"Oh, Humphie!" said little Miles eagerly, holding up the book, "*can* you remember what she used to say about this picture?"

But Humphrey taxed his memory in vain. It was all so dim, so confused, he could not remember sufficiently clearly to tell the story, so Jane was called upon to read it.

Now Jane left out her h's, and did not mind her stops, so the beautiful story of the raising of Lazarus must have lost much of its charm; but still the children listened with attention, for those who have nothing better must put up with what they have. Poor little

24

opening minds, depending thus early on the instructions of an ignorant housemaid! forced to forego, in the first budding of youth, those lessons in Divine truth that came so lovingly, and withal so forcibly, from the lips of a tender mother; those lessons which linger on the heart of the full-grown man long after the lips that pronounced them are silenced for ever.

Depend upon it, association has a great power, and those passages in the Bible which bring to children most clearly the image of their mother, are those which, in after life, are loved and valued most.

And surely those childish memories owe *something* of their charm to the recollection of the quiet, well-modulated reading, the clear, refined enunciation; the repose of the attitude in the sofa or chair, the white hand that held the book, with, it may be, the flashing of the diamond ring in the light, as the fingers turned over the pages!

Even as I write, I see rising from the darkness before me a vision of a mother and a child. I see the soft eyes meeting those of the little listener on the stool, at her knee. I see the earnestness pervading every line of the beautiful face. I almost hear the tones of the gentle voice, which, while reducing the mysteries of Divine truth to the level of the baby comprehension, carry with them the unmistakable impress of her own belief in the things of which she is telling: the certainty that the love and trust she is describing are no mere abstract truths to her, but that they are life of her life, and breath of her breath!

And I see the child's eyes glow and expand under her earnestness, as the little mind catches a refraction of her enthusiasm. Is this a picture or is it a reality? Have I brought up to any one a dimly-remembered vision? Or is it purely idealistic and fanciful?

I do not know; and even as I gaze, the picture has melted into the darkness from which I conjured it, and I see it no more!

"Boys," sounded Sir Everard's voice at the bottom of the nursery stairs, "your uncle and I are going out for a walk. No one need come with us who would rather not."

There could be but one answer to such an appeal, and a rush and scamper ensued.

It was the usual Sunday afternoon routine, the stables and the farm, and then across the meadows to inspect the hayricks, and through the corn-fields to a certain gate that commanded the finest view on the estate.

"If only this weather lasts another fortnight," said Sir Everard, as his eyes wandered over golden fields, "I think we shall have a good harvest, eh, Charlie?"

"I am sure we shall," came from Humphrey, who always had an opinion on every subject, and never lost an opportunity of obtruding it on public attention; "we shall have such a lot of corn we shan't know what to do with it."

"Well, I have never found that to be the case yet," said his father; "but if the first part of your prediction prove true, we will have a Harvest Home and a dance, and you and Miles shall lead off, 'Up the middle and down again,' with the prettiest little girls you can find in the village."

"I know who I shall dance with," said Humphrey, balancing himself on the top of the gate, "but she's not a little girl, she's quite old, nearly twenty I daresay, and she's not pretty either. I don't care to dance with little girls, its babyish."

"Who is the happy lady, Humphrey?" asked Uncle Charlie.

"She is not a lady at all," said Humphrey, indignantly, "she's Dolly, the laundry maid, and wears pattens and turned up sleeves, and her arms are as red as her cheeks. Dolly's not the least like a lady."

"Except on Sundays," put in little Miles, "because then she's got her sleeves down, and is very smart. I saw Dolly going to church this morning, with boots all covered with little white buttons."

"*That* does not make her a lady," said the elder boy contemptuously. "It is no use trying to explain to you, Miles, what a lady is because you never see any."

"Not Mrs. Jones, the steward's wife?" suggested Miles timidly, and feeling he was treading on dangerous ground.

"No," said Humphrey, "she's not a real lady, not what I call a lady. You see, Miles," he added, sinking his voice, and drawing nearer to his brother, so that he might not be overheard, "I shall never be able to make you understand, because you can't remember mother."

"No," said poor little Miles, meekly, "I suppose not."

This argument was, as he knew by experience, conclusive, and he was always completely silenced by it.

"And who will my little Miles choose for a partner?" broke in Sir Everard; "it must be some very small girl, I think."

"I should like the little girl at the lodge, please, father, because she's the very only little girl I know who is smaller than me."

"Very well: then you are both provided. Charlie, you must come down to the Harvest Home, and see 'Up the middle and down again;' Humphrey struggling with his substantial partner, and Miles bringing up the rear with the 'very only little girl he knows who is smaller than him.'" The father's eye rested smiling on his two children as he pictured the sight to himself.

"And when may it be?" asked Humphrey. "Father, please settle a day for the harvest to begin."

"When the yellow corn is almost brown, you may settle a day for the harvest," answered his father. "I have a reaping-machine this year, and so it will soon be cut when once they begin."

"I shall come every day to these fields and see how it is getting on," said Miles.

"I know a much quicker way," said Humphrey, jumping down from the gate, and pulling up several ears of corn by the roots.

"I shall have them up in the nursery, and see them ripen every day."

27

"Why, you foolish boy," said his father, "you have picked them too soon, they will never ripen now."

Humphrey looked ruefully at his ears of corn. "I quite forgot," said he.

"They will never ripen now," repeated little Miles, sorrowfully.

"Never mind, Miles," said Humphrey, "I will plant them in the sunniest part of our own garden, where the soil is much better than here, and where, I daresay, they will grow much finer and better than if they had been left to ripen with the rest. Perhaps they will thank me some day for having pulled them up out of the rough field, and planted them in such a more beautiful place."

"Perhaps they will," breathed little Miles, clasping his hands with pleasure at the idea.

Miles was leaning against the gate, looking up admiringly at his brother, and Humphrey was sitting on the topmost bar, with the ears of corn in his hand.

"Let us go," said Sir Everard, suddenly; "it is intensely hot here, and I am longing to get under those limes in the next field."

The little boys climbed over the gate, and ran on to the indicated spot, followed more leisurely by their elders.

Sir Everard and Uncle Charlie threw themselves down on the grass in the shade, and the children, seating themselves by their father, begged for a story.

"Sailors are the men for stories," was his answer; "you had better ask your uncle."

Uncle Charlie proved a charming story teller. He told them of sharks and crocodiles, of boar-hunting, and of wonderful adventures by land and sea.

The children hung on his every word.

The shadows grew long, and the sun began to sink over the cornfields, and still they were absorbed in listening, and their father in watching their sparkling eyes and varying countenances.

"Come," said Sir Everard at last, jumping up, "no more stories, or we shall be here all night. It is past six, and Virginie will be wondering what has become of us."

"Oh!" said Humphrey, drawing a long breath, as he descended from those heights of wonder to the trifling details of everyday life, recalled by the mention of Virginie, "how delicious it has been! I hope, father, you will let me be a sailor when I grow up?"

"Well, I don't think that will exactly be your vocation," answered Sir Everard; "but there is plenty of time before you."

"Me, too," said little Miles; "I want to be a sailor too."

"You, my darling," said Sir Everard, fondly; "no, not you; I couldn't spare you my sweet little fellow."

And he stooped, as he spoke, to kiss the little face that was uplifted so pleadingly to his, the lips that were always so ready to respond to his caresses.

Humphrey had turned away his head, and was gazing intently at his ears of corn.

"Is he jealous, I wonder?" thought Uncle Charlie, peering at the little face under the straw hat, and wondering whether it was a tear he saw shining among the long dark eyelashes.

But before he could make up his mind if it were so, the child's eyes were sparkling with excitement over a curious creature with a thousand legs, which had crawled out of the corn in his hand.

"And now jump up, boys, and come home." Sir Everard, as he spoke, picked up his cane, and taking his brother-in-law's arm, walked slowly on. "We shall have all these feats reproduced, Charlie, of that I am quite sure. Virginie has a nice time before her."

There was very little tea eaten that evening, the children were in such a hurry to get down again to the delectable anecdotes.

But Sir Everard took alarm at Miles's flushed cheeks and bright eyes, and would allow no more exciting stories so close upon bed-time.

"Will you finish about the crocodile to-morrow?" asked Humphrey, creeping up his uncle's leg, as he came to wish him good-night.

"To-morrow I go, my boy," he answered.

"Going to-morrow!" said Humphrey. "What a very short visit!"

"What a very short visit!" echoed Miles, who always thought it incumbent on him to say the same thing as his brother.

"I will pay you a longer visit next time," said Uncle Charlie, as he kissed the two little faces.

"But when will next time be?" persisted Humphrey.

"Yes! when will next time be?" repeated Miles.

"Ah! when indeed?" said Uncle Charlie.

———————————

CHAPTER III.

"I have got so many plans in my head, that I think I shall burst," said Humphrey to Miles the next morning, as they stood on the door-steps, watching the dog-cart vanishing in the distance, on its way to the station, with their father and uncle. "Some of the things Uncle Charlie was telling us about would be quite easy for us to do. You wouldn't be afraid, I suppose, to climb up the big tree overhanging the pond where the water-lilies are?"

"No," said Miles, rather doubtfully, "not if you went on first and gave me your hand: but that tree is a long way off—wouldn't one of the trees in the orchard do?"

"Oh, no! it wouldn't be half the fun. Don't you remember the man in the story crawled along the branch that stretched over the water? Well, this tree has a branch hanging right over the pond; and I want to crawl along it, like he did."

"Hadn't we better ask Virginie if we may go all that way alone?" suggested Miles, in the vain hope of putting off the evil moment.

Humphrey, however, did not see the force of this argument, and so they started off.

It was a very hot day, and after they had got out of the farm-yard there was no shade at all.

Humphrey skipped through the meadows and over the gates, and Miles followed him as quickly as he could, but the sun was very hot on his head, and he soon got wearied and fell back.

Humphrey did not perceive how languidly his little brother was following him, till a faint cry from behind reached him.

"Humphie, *please* stop; I can't keep up to you."

Instantly he ran back.

"I'm *so* tired, Humphie, and *so* hot, shall we go home?"

31

"Go home! why we are close to the pond now. Look, Miles, it is only across that meadow, and the corn-field beyond."

Miles followed the direction of his brother's finger, and his eye rested ruefully on the expanse lying before him, where the sun was scorching up everything.

"I'll try, Humphie," he said, resignedly.

"I tell you what!" exclaimed Humphrey, "I'll *carry* you!"

Miles felt a little nervous at the prospect, but he did not like to object.

"Just get over the gate," continued Humphrey, "and then I'll carry you across the field, and we'll soon be by the pond, where it will be as cool as possible."

Over the gate they scrambled, and then the elder boy disposed himself to take his little brother in his arms. How shall I describe the intense discomfort of the circumstances under which Miles now found himself!

One of Humphrey's arms was so tightly round his neck, that he almost felt as if he were choking, and the hand of the other grasped one of his legs with a gripe which amounted almost to pain; and *still* there was a feeling of insecurity about his position which, already very strong while Humphrey was standing still, did not diminish when he began to move.

Humphrey started with a run, but his speed soon slackened, and grave doubts began to arise even in his own mind as to the accomplishment of the task he had undertaken.

However, he staggered on. But when presently his long-suffering load began to show signs of slipping, Humphrey tightened his grasp to such a degree, that Miles, who till now had endured in silence, could endure no longer, and he uttered a faint cry for mercy.

At the same moment, Humphrey caught his foot in a rabbit hole, and both boys rolled over together. Peals of laughter from

Humphrey followed the catastrophe, but Miles did not quite enter into the spirit of the joke. He was hot and tired, poor little fellow, and began to implore his brother to take him under the neighboring hedge to rest.

Humphrey readily consented, and led him out of the baking sun.

"Perhaps we had better give it up," said he, sighing, as he sat down by Miles in the shade, "and try again in the cool of the evening. You could do it, couldn't you, if it were not for the heat?"

"Oh, yes," said Miles, eagerly. With a respite in view, he was ready to agree to anything.

"Very well," said Humphrey, "then we'll give it up and come again this evening after tea. I declare," he added, suddenly breaking off, "there's a mushroom out there!"

He was off in a moment, and returned in triumph. "Isn't it a lovely one, Miles? How fresh it smells and how beautiful it peels. If father were at home, we'd have had it cooked for his dinner, he *is* so fond of mushrooms."

"It wouldn't keep good till Friday, I suppose, for the wild men's dinner party?" enquired Miles.

"One would be no use," answered Humphrey, "but we might come here some morning and get a lot if we brought a basket. I'll tell you what, we'll get up *quite, quite* early to-morrow, and come and have a regular mushroom hunt. Won't it be fun!"

"I'm afraid Virginie would not be awake to dress me," observed Miles.

"Oh, never mind Virginie!" said Humphrey, "I'll dress you, Miles; I don't think Virginie would care to get up so early, and it would be a pity to wake her, poor thing! She goes to bed late, and is *so* tired in the morning."

"So she is, poor thing!" said Miles.

33

"And besides, you know," continued Humphrey, "she always thinks something dreadful will happen if she doesn't come with us, and it would be a pity to frighten her for nothing."

"So it would; a great pity," repeated Miles. "But what's that noise, Humphie? Is it a cock crowing or a bull roaring?"

Both children listened.

There was many a sound to be heard round about on that summer morning; the buzzing of bees as they flitted about among the clover, the chirrup of the grasshoppers in the long grass, the crowing of a cock from the farm, and the lowing of cattle in the distance, but that which had attracted Miles' attention was none of all these. It was the gradually approaching sound of a female voice, which, as its owner neared the meadow, assumed to the two little listeners the familiar tones of the French language.

"M. Humphrey! M. Miles! M. Humphrey! où êtes-vous donc?"

"It's Virginie!" they both exclaimed, jumping up.

Virginie it was; and great was the horror she expressed at their having strayed so far from home, at the state of heat in which she found Miles, and at his having been taken such a long walk.

Many were the reproaches she heaped upon Humphrey as they walked back to the house for having caused *her* such a hunt in the heat of the sun, and her nerves such a shock as they had experienced when she had not found him and his brother in their usual haunts.

Lastly she brought him up with the inquiry, "Et vos leçons! Savez vous qu'il est midi passé?"

Humphrey's ideas of time were always of the vaguest order, and when anything of so exciting a nature as this morning's expedition came in the way, hours *were* not in his calculations.

He did not mend matters much by saying he should have thought it had been about half-past nine.

Virginie maintained a dignified silence after this explanation, till they reached the hall door; and it now being too near dinner time to make it worth while for Humphrey to get out his books, she informed him that he would have to do all his lessons in the afternoon.

This was perhaps more of a punishment to Miles than to Humphrey.

Lessons were no trouble to Humphrey when once his attention was fixed on them; and if it were not for the penance of having to sit still in a chair, he did not really dislike them. But to Miles, his brother's lesson hours were times of dreary probation. He was not allowed to speak to him, or distract his attention in any way; and had to sit turning over the leaves of a picture book, or building a solitary castle of bricks, in some part of the room where Humphrey could not see him without regularly turning his head round.

Humphrey made a faint attempt after dinner to persuade Virginie to let him do his lessons in the garden, under the big tree on the lawn; but it was instantly negatived. In the nursery, with his back turned to Miles, she did sometimes succeed in concentrating his attention on his reading; but she knew too much of the all-powerful attractions out of doors to comply with his proposal. Not to mention the chance of Carlo suddenly jumping upon the book, or the tempting vicinity of the gardeners with the mowing machine, there was always risk to his powers of attention in chance butterflies and humble bees, the dropping of a blossom from the tree above, or the sudden advent of a stray water-wag-tail.

Humphrey did not press the question, and opened his book with a slight sigh, for which Virginie could not account.

Was there a memory floating in the child's mind of a time when the same request had never been made in vain?—of summer afternoons, dimly remembered, when, sitting by his mother's side under the same old tree, he had learnt to read words of one syllable out of the baby primer on her knee?—and when, if his attention *had* sometimes wandered to the summer sights and sounds around him, her gentle "Now, my darling try and attend to your reading," would instantly recall it. And then the quick shutting up of the book when the specified stage had been reached, the fond kiss of dismissal, and the joyous "Now run away, my child, and play to your heart's content!" as if she rejoiced as much as he did that he should be released from his temporary bondage, and disport himself in the sunshine once more!

Great stillness now reigned in the nursery for more than an hour. It was only broken by the monotonous drone of Humphrey's reading, and Virginie's occasional "Tenez-vous bien. Otez donc les bras de la table Ne donnez pas des coups de pied à la chaise"— varied by the fall of Miles's bricks, as he knocked down one completed castle after another, in despair at not being able to call upon his brother to admire them.

As the time at which Humphrey's release was due approached, and there were no signs of moving on Virginie's part, Miles gave vent, at intervals, to deep-drawn sighs.

It came at last; Virginie shut up the book, and put a mark in it, and Humphrey, with a loud "Hurrah," dashed his chair suddenly back, and turned head over heels on the floor.

Miles threw himself upon him, and the two rolled over and over each other, in the "abandon" of perfect enjoyment.

"We'll start for the pond directly after tea," whispered Humphrey.

But Virginie had other plans in view, and to the children's disgust they were taken for a walk with her, to visit the wife of one of the farmers.

The long confinement in the farmer's kitchen, while Virginie and the farmer's wife talked about bonnets and trimmings, was very wearisome to the two boys. Miles found some compensation in the discovery of a tiny kitten on the hearth; and Humphrey, mounting on a chair, played with the trigger of the farmer's gun which hung over the mantelpiece, "just to see whether it was loaded or not."

They did not get home till Miles's bed-time.

Humphrey established himself on the edge of the bath, and watched Virginie carefully as she undressed his little brother, that he might learn how Miles's vestments succeeded each other; for he felt a little doubtful of his own powers as a valet.

His face lengthened considerably when he saw how many strings there would be to tie.

He drew nearer, in his eagerness, as Virginie untied them one after the other; and began considering how to do the untying process backwards, and wondering whether it would produce the desired result.

"Don't be in such a hurry," he called out, in his excitement, as she pulled out the last tie, "I didn't half see."

Virginie's look of astonishment recalled him to himself, and he retreated hastily to his seat on the edge of the bath.

Fortunately for him, she was so taken up with reproving him for speaking to her in English, that she forgot to inquire into his extraordinary interest in the tape strings.

CHAPTER IV.

Little Miles was dreaming on a green bank, on the top of which he and Humphrey were seated, making daisy-chains, when suddenly the midges began to fly in his face in a most disagreeable manner. Buzz, buzz, they came up against his cheeks like hard lumps, and he couldn't drive them away. He turned to Humphrey for assistance, and such a strong gust of wind blew upon one side of his head and face that he fell over on his side and began to slip down the hill. He clutched hold of his brother to save himself, and woke—to find neither bank nor daisies but that Humphrey was dragging him out of bed.

"At last!" whispered Humphrey. "I thought you never *were* going to wake. I've tried *everything*! I've thrown bits of biscuit in your face, I've blown into your ear, I've shaken you till I was tired; I couldn't speak, you know, for fear of waking Virginie. Be very quiet, for she's moved once or twice."

"But what do you want, Humphie?" asked Miles, rubbing his eyes. "Why do you get out of bed in the middle of the night?"

"Middle of the night!" echoed Humphrey, "why it's broad daylight! Look at the hole in the shutter, how sunny it is out of doors. I've been lying awake ever since the cock crew, watching the light get brighter and brighter, and——"

But before he had concluded his sentence his weary little brother had settled himself again on his pillow.

"Miles! Miles!" whispered Humphrey in despair, stooping over him.

"Good night, Humphie," said Miles, sleepily.

"Why, you're going to sleep again," said Humphrey in his ear.

"No, I'm not," said the child, dreamily.

"Yes, you are!" exclaimed Humphrey, forgetting, in his excitement, that he was speaking out loud.

"No, I'm not," repeated Miles, trying to seem very wide-awake: but the fringed eyelids drooped over the heavy eyes, and he tried to keep them open in vain.

An ominous stir from the big bed prevented Humphrey from answering, and he watched Virginie nervously, as she rolled over from one side to the other.

Miles took advantage of the pause and fell asleep again directly.

"Wake up! wake up!" said Humphrey, returning to the charge.

Miles sat up in bed.

"What *is* the matter, Humphie?"

"Nothing's the matter, but don't you remember our *delicious* plan to get up early and pick mushrooms?"

Miles remembered now, but the plan did not seem so delicious now, somehow, as it had done the day before.

"Get up now, Humphie?" he said dejectedly.

"Yes," answered his energetic brother, "you won't mind it when we're once out in the fields. I'm going to dress you before I dress myself, so be quick and jump up. You'll feel all right when you're out of bed."

Little Miles looked half inclined to cry.

"I'm so sleepy," he said wistfully.

"You'll be better soon," said Humphrey, pulling off the bed-clothes.

"Let's go to-morrow instead, Humphie." Humphrey had turned round to get Miles's boots and stockings, and did not hear this last proposal. When he came back to the bed-side, to his horror, Miles had lain down again.

"What is to be done?" he exclaimed in despair. A sudden thought struck him, and he went quickly off to the other end of the room.

Miles was not quite asleep, and attracted by a clatter, he raised himself to see what his brother was about.

"What are you going to do, Humphie?" he exclaimed, as he saw Humphrey coming slowly across the room with a great jug of water in his arms.

"Why you see," said Humphrey in a loud whisper, and rather out of breath, for he was oppressed by the weight of the water jug, "the best way to wake people is to pour a jug of cold water suddenly on their face, and so——"

"Oh! I'm quite awake now, Humphie; indeed," interrupted Miles, getting out of bed in a great hurry, "you needn't, really. Look at my eyes." And in great trepidation the child opened his large blue eyes to their fullest extent.

Humphrey was satisfied, and put the jug down. Miles would have been happier to see it safely replaced on the distant wash-hand stand, and offered to help to carry it back, if his brother found it too heavy.

He was not much reassured by Humphrey's answer:

"It'll do very well there; and, besides, it's better to have it near, in case you get sleepy again."

The toilette now began in earnest: Humphrey gave Miles his stockings to put on while he proceeded to dress himself, and was all ready but his jacket, when turning round he found Miles in great perplexity, with his toe unaccountably fixed in the place where his heel ought to be.

"I can't get it out, Humphie!"

"I must do it, I suppose," said the elder boy; and he seized the leg, nearly upsetting Miles as he did so, and proceeded to put on the stocking wrong side out.

40

"It doesn't matter the least," he assured Miles, who was rather discomfited at the bits of thread, and general unfinished appearance of his leg. But what *did* matter was, that the walking-boots had not, of course, come up from being cleaned.

"Never mind," said Humphrey; "shoes will do."

On came the delicate child's thin in-door shoes, without any reference to the heavy dew and long grass attendant upon mushroom hunting. Miles was then divested of his night-gown, and his under-clothes put on.

All went on smoothly till the first tying of strings, and here Humphrey was completely at fault. It was no use.

"Don't you think you could hold all your things together?" he suggested; "and then I'll pop on your blouse quick, and make the band very tight, to keep it all steady?"

Miles agreed to this plan, as he did to all others, more especially as he found the alternative was the insertion of a huge pin, with which Humphrey offered to "make it all comfortable!"

"I don't know how it is," said little Miles, shaking himself about, "but I don't feel as warm as usual."

"Don't shake like that, Miles," exclaimed Humphrey; "it'll all come down, you know. Get your hat, and let's come along quietly."

"Why! I have had no bath!" said Miles, stopping short.

"No more have I," echoed Humphrey, "I quite forgot! And what's this?" he added, picking up a small flannel shirt.

"Why, it's mine," said Miles.

"So it is," rejoined Humphrey, "of course; that's why you felt cold. Well, we can't wait now. Come along: be very quiet." And the two boys stepped quietly out of the room, and of course left the door wide open behind them.

It was not much more than half-past five by the clock in the hall, and doors and windows were as yet all barred. The light came in fitfully through any chinks or holes it could find, and gave a generally mysterious aspect to the hall and staircase. Little Miles glanced rather timidly round, and drew nearer to his brother, as they passed through the library and billiard-room, as if the unwonted appearance of the familiar apartments threw something of the supernatural round about them.

Any one who has risen at an unusual hour, and come into the sitting-rooms before the household is stirring, will understand something of the child's feeling. The chairs and tables are undergoing a phase which to them is familiar, but which is quite strange to us.

We only know them as in connection with ourselves, and do not dream that they have an existence in which we are not, with which we have nothing to do. We know them in the busy day and in the lighted room at night; but with the grey dawn creeping in upon them they are quite strangers, and even mysterious.

Hans Christian Andersen recognized and expressed this feeling when he laid the scene of one of his fairy tales in a drawing-room at dead of night, and endowed the inanimate objects in the room with the attributes of human beings.

The two little brothers found their way out by the conservatory, and went to the tool-house to fetch some baskets, before setting out for the mushroom fields.

The dew was heavy on flowers and grass and when they got into the meadow, their feet, and legs got very wet.

At sight of the first batch of mushrooms in the distance, Humphrey got wild, and with a scream of joy he bounded towards it. From one batch to another he sped, picking as fast as he could, and was soon out of sight.

Humphrey had it all to himself, for Miles could not keep up, and he was soon left far behind with his basket. He was a little disconcerted at first, when he saw Humphrey gradually getting further and further away; but having satisfied himself by a hasty glance round the field, that there were no bulls near, he became reconciled to his solitude, and began to fill his basket, humming a little tune to himself as he did so.

He was rather surprised, as he went along, to see how many mushrooms Humphrey had left untouched. They were such lovely ones too! all red and yellow outside, and white inside, and so huge!

He filled his basket with them in great triumph, and then sat down under a tree to wait for Humphrey's return.

The early morning air was rather fresh, and he began to feel a little cold without his flannel shirt. His feet, too, were very wet, and he got up to take a little run to warm himself. He caught sight of Humphrey coming towards him, and ran to meet him.

"Oh, Humphie! I've got such a lot, and such beauties! Come and see them under the tree."

"Look here!" said Humphrey, holding up his basket; "did you ever see such a quantity?"

Miles looked a little nervously at the white exteriors of Humphrey's mushrooms.

"Mine are quite different, Humphie."

"You haven't been picking fungus, I hope?" exclaimed Humphrey, stopping short.

"Oh, no!" said Miles, quickly—"at least I don't think I have," he added doubtfully, "But what *is* fungus, Humphie?"

"Toadstools," answered Humphrey, "horrid big yellow toads; there are lots of them about in the fields. Where are they, Miles? Show them to me, quick!"

"They're under the trees," said Miles; and both boys set off running.

"Toads, every one!" proclaimed Humphrey, emptying the basket on the ground. "Not one mushroom in the lot. Why, Miles! do you know they're poison?"

Miles stood aghast—the awe of the announcement completely softening the disappointment.

"It's lucky I saw them before they were cooked," continued Humphrey, in a tone of great solemnity; "fancy, if all the wild men had been poisoned! It would have been your fault."

"Oh, Humphie!" said little Miles, in terror, "let's throw them away."

"We'll smash them," said Humphrey; "and that'll do as well."

So they made a heap of the fungus, and stamped upon them till their shoes and stockings were covered with the nasty compound.

"What will Virginie say?" laughed Humphrey, as he looked at his legs.

"What *will* she say?" echoed Miles, delighted. Suddenly he stopped short. "Humphie! I never said my prayers!"

"Good gracious! No more have I."

"What shall we do? We shall have to go home. It wouldn't be right, I suppose, to say them out of doors?"

"No harm at all," said Humphrey; "let's say them under the tree."

And, suiting the action to the word, with his usual promptitude, Humphrey knelt down; but he was up again directly.

"I was going to tell you, Miles, that we'd better take off our hats while we say them; every one does when they go to church; which, of course, you don't know, as you're too young to go there."

Miles received the information with great respect, and began to disentangle his elastic from his hair.

"Not yet!" exclaimed Humphrey; "wait till we kneel down; I'll tell you when."

Miles kept his eyes fixed upon Humphrey, with his hand on the brim of his hat, ready to take it off at the expected signal.

"Now!" said Humphrey. Down knelt the two little brothers on the grass, baring their curly heads as they did so.

Little Miles was accustomed to repeat his prayer after Virginie, and did not know it by heart; and he was in great perplexity till Humphrey had finished, not knowing whether it would be best to remain kneeling or not.

In about five minutes Humphrey jumped up and put on his hat. Miles rose too, and confided his troubles. Humphrey instantly gave the subject his earnest attention.

"It would never do for you to say my prayer after me," he said, reflectively; "you're too young."

"Too young," repeated Miles, meekly.

"And I've forgotten my baby prayer, *of course*," continued Humphrey; "it's so very very long since I used to say it—— I'll tell you what, Miles, you might say your grace!"

"My grace?" said Miles, rather scared; "why, that isn't prayers, is it, Humphie?"

"Oh, yes, it is," answered Humphrey; "in your little book of 'Prayers for Children,' your grace has got at the top of it, 'A prayer after meat.' Meat, you know, means breakfast, dinner, and tea; even if you only have bread and butter, or sop."

"*Does* it?" exclaimed Miles. "I thought meat was only beef and mutton—hardly chicken!"

"Ah! but it does, though," said Humphrey, in a superior tone; "you don't know, Miles. There's lots of things you don't know yet. Why you thought grace wasn't prayers, and yet it is. Now say this after me: 'For what I have received, may the Lord make me truly thankful.'"

"Why! that's *your* grace, Humphie, not *mine*! Mine is only, 'Thank God for my good breakfast.'"

"That will do," said Humphrey.

"But, Humphie! I've not *had* my breakfast! How can I say it?"

"To be sure," said Humphrey, reflectively, "that makes it very awkward. You've not even had a bit of bread. If you'd only had a biscuit, it would have done—it's very unlucky."

He remained for some minutes in an attitude of deep thought.

"I know!" he exclaimed suddenly; "I always say a grace *before* my meals, and of course you'll have some breakfast presently, so you can say my grace after me. It's very difficult for you, of course; but still, if I say it very slowly, you can manage to do it. Now listen very attentively: 'For what I am going to receive, may the Lord make me truly thankful.'"

Miles knelt down and repeated the little prayer, and then the two little brothers sat down on the grass, and counted their mushrooms, to see how' many there would be for the wild men apiece.

Meanwhile Virginie, awakened by the rush of cold air caused by the open door, sat up in bed and looked about her.

The two little nightgowns on the floor and the jug of water in the middle of the room, first attracted her attention; but the room being partially dark, she did not perceive that the children had disappeared. She got up and opened the shutters, and then stood staring at the empty beds, the sheets and blankets scattered in all directions. And then she advanced hurriedly to Humphrey's bed, to see if the children were hidden beneath it. She looked also under the wardrobe, behind the curtains, in the toy cupboard. But her astonishment changed to alarm when she found their clothes were missing, and she ran into the day-nursery, and hung over the stairs shouting, "M. Humphrey! M. Miles!"

Not being dressed, she could not go down, so she rang the bell violently, and began to put on her things as quickly as she could.

The housemaid who answered the bell could give no account of the young gentlemen, but volunteered to search the house for them.

While she was absent Virginie's eyes fell on Miles's flannel shirt, and she wrung her hands in despair.

"They must have gone out," said the housemaid, returning; "the conservatory door is wide open, and so is the outer door."

"Impossible!" stuttered Virginie, in her broken English; "their walking boots have not mounted; they have not but the thin shoes of the house!"

"They must be out," repeated the housemaid, "for I've hunted every corner. Have they taken their hats?"

Virginie strode across the room, and opened a drawer.

"Mon Dieu!" she exclaimed, when she saw it was empty.

"But, I say," she continued, gesticulating violently with both hands, "that M. Miles will catch the cold, the cough, the croup. See there, Jeanne! he has not the flannel shirt he carries always. His chest will inflame. He will die!"

She began to put on her bonnet.

"There they are!" exclaimed Jane, who had gone to the window. "Look there! out in that field!"

"In the fields? sitting on the wet grass!" said Virginie in horror, as she distinguished the two little figures in the distance, seated under a tree. "Entrez, entrez, à l'instant!" she screamed to the children, though they were much too far off to hear. She seized her shawl and ran down-stairs.

The little boys were coming homewards when she got into the garden, and she hurried on to meet them. Miles had hold of his brother's hand, and was walking rather wearily; but Humphrey,

47

with his head still full of the success of his morning sport, disregarded alike Miles's languor and Virginie's infuriated appearance.

"Regardez!" he shouted in triumph, holding up his basket of mushrooms.

At the sight of Miles's wet boots and flushed cheeks, Virginie forgot all the reproaches she had prepared for Humphrey and merely with lofty disdain confiscating his mushrooms, she took Miles up in her arms and carried him home.

Humphrey trotted along by her side, entreating to have his basket restored, but she took no notice of him.

She carried Miles straight up into the nursery, and began to undress him. He presented a curious appearance when his blouse was taken off—strings all knotted together, buttons forced into the wrong holes, and hooks clinging to outlets that were never intended for them.

Miles yawned all the time, and sneezed once or twice, each time provoking from Virginie an exclamation, half of alarm and half of anger.

"You needn't scold Miles," called out Humphrey, who was being washed in the distance by the nursery-maid; "he didn't want to come—it was all me."

When they were dressed again, the two little culprits were seated to their breakfast, but forbidden to hold any communication with each other except in French.

It was rather a slow ending to so pleasant a beginning, especially as after breakfast Miles was so tired that he had to lie down, and Humphrey was hardly allowed to move for fear of disturbing him.

Virginie would not let them out of her sight for the rest of the day, and they took a dull walk in the afternoon, one on each side of her.

Towards evening, Miles gave forth an ominous cough, and was decidedly croupy at night.

Virginie's nerves always deserted her when the delicate boy was ill in his father's absence, and towards the middle of the next day she could stand it no longer, and sent off for the doctor.

Humphrey was very remorseful when Virginie informed him it was his fault that Miles was unwell, and remained in a state of great depression for about three minutes. But the sight of the doctor's gig coming up the avenue sent it all out of his head, and he dashed down-stairs, three steps at a time, to receive him at the hall door.

"Well, Doctor," he called out; "how are you? Why, you've got new harness to your horse! How jolly and clean it looks."

"New harness?—yes," said the doctor, dismounting; "but tell me what's the matter with your brother?"

"Oh, it was the mushrooms," said Humphrey, vaguely, and with his eyes running over the new reins and straps. "I wonder how long they'll look so fresh and clean?"

"Mushrooms!" exclaimed the doctor; "you don't mean to say they let that delicate child eat mushrooms? Has he got an attack of indigestion?"

"Oh, no," said Humphrey, springing down the steps and patting the horse; "a pain in his chest, I think. How glossy his coat is to-day, isn't it?"

"Same thing—same thing," said the doctor; "and I'm sure I don't wonder, if they let him eat mushrooms."

Humphrey burst out laughing, having for the first time given his attention to what the doctor was saying.

"Why, they were raw!" he said.

"Raw mushrooms!" exclaimed the doctor, "who could have allowed him to eat them?"

"But he didn't eat any," said Humphrey, convulsed. And he rolled about so, as he laughed at the doctor's mistake, that he knocked up against the horse, who immediately plunged.

"Take care, my dear child," said the doctor, pulling him away; "you mustn't frighten black Bob—he won't stand it. But, tell me," he continued, drawing the boy into the hall, "Why did you say the mushrooms had given him a pain in his chest?"

"It was the flannel shirt——" began Humphrey; but at the sound of hoofs on the gravel outside, he broke off suddenly: "Oh there's black Bob plunging again; I *must* go and see—let me go, please." He broke from the doctor's grasp, and ran back to the door, calling out as he did so: "It might have been the flannel shirt, perhaps, if it wasn't the shoes; but we were in such a hurry."

Despairing of getting any sense out of him, the doctor let him go, and pursued his way up-stairs, where he had full details from Virginie.

He did not think Miles very bad, but ordered him to be kept in two rooms for the rest of the week.

I need hardly say that when he came down again Humphrey had persuaded the groom to let him get into the gig, and there he was in the broiling sun without his hat, driving black Bob round and round the approach.

CHAPTER V.

Little Miles was terribly disappointed to find his confinement up-stairs would extend over the day of the dinner-party, but there was no help for it.

The eventful Friday arrived, and Humphrey was on the fidget all day. He paid constant visits to the dining-room and library, and even intruded into the kitchen; but he could see nothing in any of the preparations going on which at all differed from those usual.

"I suppose, for once they will eat like civilized people," he told Miles—after visit one hundred and fourth down-stairs, in the vain hope of finding something new.

"Yes, just for a treat," suggested little Miles; and they amused themselves for the next few hours by imagining the astonishment of the wild men at all the different things they would see.

Sir Everard arrived late, and went straight up to Miles's room. It so happened that he did not see Humphrey, as he was under the hands of Virginie, in preparation for his appearance in company; and as several of the guests had already arrived, Sir Everard had only just time to kiss Miles, and to hurry off to his dressing-room, from whence he descended to the library. So that the conversation of the preceding week, and the children's excitement over the prospect of the aborigines, had entirely escaped his memory, for want of the refreshing it would have been sure to have received had he had time for a word with either of his little boys.

He was deep in politics with an old gentleman in a broad expanse of satin waistcoat, and a general buzz of conversation was going on all over the room, when the library door was flung open with a bounce, and Humphrey appeared in the doorway.

Fresh from Virginie's improving hand, in velveteen clothes, white waistcoat, and light blue tie, with his brown hair brushed back from his bright face, and his eyes sparkling with excitement, he looked like a being of another sphere, among the rusty old gentlemen congregated in the room.

Many of them turned round to look at the pretty boy, and more than one held out a hand of greeting.

But, to Sir Everard's annoyance, Humphrey, whose manners were usually perfect, took not the slightest notice of any of these overtures.

He stood at the door as if spell-bound, gazing around him with an expression of intense surprise, wonder, and disappointment.

"Humphrey," said Sir Everard, "why don't you come and say 'How do you do?' to these gentlemen?"

"Father," exclaimed the boy, in a clear treble voice, that was heard all over the room, "where are the wild men?"

The ghastly truth flashed across Sir Everard's mind, as the boy asked the question. The recollection of the children's conversation with their uncle came back to him, and he was at his wit's end.

"Wild men, Humphrey?" he said, with a sickly smile, "what are you dreaming about? There are no wild men here."

"You know what I mean, father," the child answered, in the same clear voice, making his way straight across the room to Sir Everard; "the wild men of the woods, that you and Uncle Charlie were talking about last Saturday, and who you said you were going to have to dinner. There were two long words, and the one I mean—means wild men. It was a very long word, the a—abo——"

"Constituents?" gasped the baronet.

Fortunately for Sir Everard's seat in Parliament, the two long words, heard for the first time that Saturday, had confused themselves in the boy's mind, and he answered "I suppose it was—but *I* thought it began with an 'a.'"

"And you thought 'constituents' meant 'wild men?'" pursued his father, eagerly following up his advantage, while the guests laughed. "Why did you not ask me, or look it out in the dictionary? Though, to be sure," concluded the baronet, appealing to the bystanders, "I don't know that it would have been easy to make it clear to a child of seven."

"No, indeed," answered one or two.

"But why should he think it meant wild men?" asked another, laughingly.

"A child's natural love of the extraordinary, I suppose," answered Sir Everard, "the unknown is always the marvellous, and ignorance is always the most easily deceived."

He hardly knew if he was talking sense or not; he only felt he must provide an answer of some kind, and having silenced his questioner, he breathed freely again. But there was an only half-satisfied expression on Humphrey's face which alarmed his father: and dreading that he should cast his thoughts back, and by raking up something else that had been said on that fatal occasion furnish to the assembled guests the clue to the conversation, he drew the boy to him, and told him he had better run back to his brother.

It still wanted five minutes to dinner; and he felt there was no peace of mind for him, as long as Humphrey remained in the room.

As if to atone for his unceremonious entry, Humphrey seemed determined that his exit should be more in accordance with the rules of society; for he advanced to the fat gentleman next his father, and holding out his hand wished him "good night;" then, proceeding to the next in order, he did likewise.

"Is he going to shake hands with every single one?" thought Sir Everard, in despair, as his eyes wandered from one to another of his twenty guests, dispersed all over the library.

There could be no doubt about it. Patiently and methodically Humphrey went through his task. Not one was overlooked—not one was left out.

No matter if one was standing apart, at the other end of the room, another deep in a volume of prints, and two more tête-à-tête in a political discussion. Humphrey thought nothing of pursuing the first, rousing the second, and disturbing the others. The inevitable "good-night" rang out all down the room, and the inevitable little palm was outstretched.

Sir Everard ever afterwards looked back to those slow moments of torture, as to a sort of hideous nightmare. Each minute was laden with anxiety, each new handshaking fraught with danger, each conversation that a guest opened with the child, a fresh source of fear.

Interminable moments! The hands of the clock seemed as if they would never move, the gong seemed as if it would never sound, and he stood in despair, watching the little figure pursuing its triumphal progress down the room, and listening to the patronizing tones in which one and the other rallied the boy on his mistake.

"So you thought you were going to see a lot of wild men, young gentleman?"

"Uncle Charlie told me so," was the answer.

Sir Everard fidgeted from one leg to the other. ("Only thirteen more," he observed to himself.)

"And you're quite disappointed?" said the next one, laughing.

"Yes," said Humphrey; "there isn't much to see in a lot of gentlemen in black coats."

("Only twelve now," reflected the baronet.)

"It was a joke of uncle's, I suppose," said a paterfamilias, in a consoling tone—and Sir Everard beat the ground nervously with his foot.

"A very stupid joke," said Humphrey, with which opinion his father fervently agreed.

It ended at last. The gong sounded, the last "good night" was said, and with an indescribable sense of relief Sir Everard saw the little figure disappear. But he did not recover himself all the evening. It was remarked that he was silent and abstracted during the dinner, and the guests shook their heads, and observed that he had never got over his wife's death. He was truly thankful when the party broke up, and the strain was over.

He could not pass the bedroom nursery without taking a look at Miles. He was sleeping peacefully, but various sounds, as if of sobbing, came from the other little bed.

Sir Everard laid his hand on the sheet, but it was held tight, and the curly head hidden beneath it. "Why, Humphrey, my little man, what is the matter?"

Very inarticulate sounds succeeded, but by dint of great patience, the baronet distinguished among the sobs that, "he was afraid Uncle Charlie would go to hell, for telling such a dreadful story, and he couldn't bear to think of it!"

CHAPTER VI.

Virginie waylaid Sir Everard on his way down to breakfast next morning, to beg him to speak to Humphrey on the subject of leading Miles into mischief.

The baronet acquiesced with a sigh. It was a job he particularly disliked. In the short time he was able to be with his children, he enjoyed seeing them all life and happiness; and he hated to bring a cloud over their bright faces.

Humphrey was hanging out of the window when his father went into the dining room, and Sir Everard was half afraid of calling him away, for fear of startling him, and causing him to fall out; but at the sound of his father's footsteps, the boy drew himself in and bounded towards him.

"Why did you not come and help me to dress this morning?" said Sir Everard, as he kissed him.

Humphrey looked rather bored. "Virginie wouldn't let me," he answered; "she thought it would be a good punishment."

Here was an opening! Sir Everard felt he ought not to let it slip.

"Punishment!" said he, trying to look very solemn; "I am sorry to hear you deserved punishing. Why, what have you been doing?"

Humphrey looked up to the ceiling, down to the ground, and all round the room. "I can't remember what it was, father!"

Sir Everard tried hard not to smile. "What is the use of scolding such a boy," thought he; "a child who does not even remember for what offence he is suffering?"

"Stop a minute!" cried Humphrey, who was still in an attitude of reflection, "perhaps I shall remember presently."

He ran over his recent misdemeanors in his head, checking them off with his fingers and his father, seeing it was likely to be a long job, sat down to breakfast.

"Well, Humphrey!" he questioned, after a pause, "have you remembered?"

"No, I *can't*," answered the boy, "but I'm sure Virginie will. Shall I run up and ask her?"

Sir Everard was amused, but a little provoked. It seemed such a hopeless task ever to make an impression upon Humphrey. But he only said, "No, you need not do that; I think I can tell you a little about it. Come and sit down here."

Sir Everard turned the tap of the urn, and put on the longest face he could think of. "I am sorry to hear from Virginie," he began, looking full at Humphrey, so as to make sure he was gaining his attention, "that you have——"

He stopped in despair, for Humphrey's eyes had wandered to the tap, and his mind was intent on the running water.

"Are you listening to me, Humphrey?"

"Take care!" was all Humphrey's answer jumping up from his chair, and clapping his hands; "turn it off! quick! look! look! father!"

There was no help for it, Sir Everard had to break off his discourse, and attend to the water, which was running all over the table, and the boy's laughter was so infectious that he joined heartily in it.

"I give it up," he said to himself; "it's no use trying to make an impression on anything so volatile."

"It served you quite right, father," said Humphrey, "for not letting me turn on the tap. You know quite well Miles and I always take turns to do it. Oh! I wish it would happen again!" And at the recollection, the merry laugh broke out once more.

But the mention of the little prisoner up-stairs, recalled Sir Everard to a sense of his duty, for Miles was suffering for his brother's thoughtlessness. So he gave Humphrey a long lecture on leading his brother astray and threatened him with the continual espionage of Virginie in the garden if he had any more complaints of the kind.

Humphrey sat looking very mournful while the discourse lasted, and was vehement in his promises that it should never happen again.

"Till next time, I suppose," said the baronet, laughing; and then he gave him some bread and honey and took up the newspaper.

He felt rather proud of the effect he had produced, for Humphrey ate his bread and honey in silence, and seemed very thoughtful.

"Boys will not attend to the maids," he reflected; "there is nothing like the authority of a parent after all."

In about five minutes, Humphrey's meditations came to a close.

"Father!"

"What, my boy," said Sir Everard, putting down the paper, in anticipation of some penitent speech, and mentally saying, "I did not mean him to take it so much to heart, poor child!"

"If you had lived in the times of the Wars of the Roses, which side would you have taken?"

Sir Everard was rather taken aback. In the first place, because it was rather a shock to his feelings to find, after all, how little impression he had made; and in the second, he was by no means so familiar with that part of history as to be able to give his opinion in a hurry. He would not, however, lower himself in the boy's estimation by allowing his ignorance.

"Wars of the Roses," he repeated, to gain a little time for reflection; "have you been learning a great deal about them lately?"

"Yes," said Humphrey, with a sigh; "Virginie seems *very* fond of them. Is it true that unless I remember all the battles of the Wars of the Roses, I shall never be able to go into parliament?"

"Does Virginie say so?" enquired Sir Everard.

"Yes," said Humphrey. "She says, of course all the members of parliament know the names at the tips of their fingers and could say them in order; and which were won by Yorkists and which by Lancastrians."

Sir Everard felt very thankful that he held his seat on less frail a tenure, and sincerely hoped his son was not going to put him to the test. Vain hope!

"I suppose, of course, father, *you* could say them right off?"

"It's almost a pity to stay indoors such a fine day," said the baronet, hastily; "suppose you get your hat and run out in the garden."

Yorkists and Lancastrians at once vanished from Humphrey's head, and he was off. But when he was gone, Sir Everard took down a volume of English History, and studied it for the rest of the morning.

After luncheon, Sir Everard proposed to take Humphrey out riding.

Little Miles looked very disconsolate when the horses came to the door, and he found himself condemned to a solitary afternoon, but seemed somewhat cheered by a long-whispered confabulation that his brother had with him before starting.

At three o'clock Sir Everard and Humphrey mounted, and as they went along the road, the following conversation took place:—

"Will you pass through the town, father; because I've got some shopping to do?"

"Shopping! why what do you want to buy?"

"It's such a very great secret, that I don't think I can tell you. But perhaps you can keep a secret?"

"Yes, I think I may promise to keep it."

"Well, then, I'll tell you. It's a birthday present for you. And what would you like? But you must promise not to tell any one."

"No one shall know: but I think I would rather you chose for me; what you like, I shall like."

"Well, now, I don't think you would. You see, *I* should like a pop-gun, or some nine-pins. Now *you* would not care for either of those, would you?"

Sir Everard admitted that he was getting a little old for these amusements.

"I thought so!" pursued Humphrey, delighted with his own discrimination, "and that's what makes it so difficult. You've got a watch and a thermometer, and all the other things grown-up men have, so it is very puzzling."

"But, my dear child, all the things you mention are very expensive, far beyond your little means, I should think. Why, how much money have you got?"

"Well! that's just the awkward part; I have not got any! But I thought perhaps you wouldn't mind giving me some, as it is for your own birthday present."

Sir Everard laughed.

"Rather an expensive way of having birthday presents."

"I don't think it will be very expensive," said the practical Humphrey; "but of course it depends on what I buy. Here is the shop, father; please stop."

They pulled up before one of those little nondescript shops to be found in every small country-town.

"Now mind," said Humphrey, as he jumped down from his pony, "mind you don't peep through the door, because you might see me looking at things on the counter."

He waited for a moment till he had exacted a promise from Sir Everard, and then ran into the shop.

"I want something for a grown-up man," he said, as he advanced to the counter.

The shop-woman did her best to show everything she thought likely to suit, but Humphrey was not at all satisfied with the choice. His restless eyes wandered all over the shop. "Have not you got anything for a man to put in his pocket?" he asked.

An inspiration seized the woman, and she advanced to the window.

"Take care!" called out Humphrey, to the woman's great surprise, as she began to take down some things.

"Please don't," he continued, in an agony, as, startled by his shout, she remained, with a compass in one hand and a purse in the other.

"Father's out there, and he'll see what you take down, and guess it's for his birthday present."

The woman humbly begged his pardon, but it was too late; Humphrey would not look at either purse or compass. "You've spoilt it all," he said; "he must have seen."

He remained leaning disconsolately against the counter, gazing with no friendly eye on the rapidly increasing heap of goods which the patient woman produced from all corners of the shop for his inspection.

"Have you got a husband?" he asked, suddenly.

To Humphrey's horror, the woman put up her apron to her eyes, and began to cry.

"Oh! I'm *so* sorry," said he; "I didn't mean to make you cry, really. I see now you've got a cap on, so of course he's dead. I'm *very* sorry he's dead," he continued after a pause, "because I was going to say perhaps he would have been able to tell me what a grown-up man would like." Then, afraid he had been unfeeling, he added, "Of course, I'm sorry too, because it seems to make you unhappy. You don't remember, I suppose," he went on, doubtfully, and eyeing the widow carefully, to see how far he might go without fear of a fresh outburst, "what he used to like for his birthday presents?"

The woman cast her thoughts back to the memory of the defunct, and the prominent idea connected with him being tobacco-smoke, she suggested a cigar-case.

Humphrey was delighted at the idea.

"You don't mean to say they're in the window!" he exclaimed in despair.

The widow was obliged to admit that it was too true.

"What are we to do!" said Humphrey, dejectedly. "I know!" he added, the next moment running to the door.

"Father!" he shouted, "would you mind turning your head away for a minute, because we're going to get something out of the window."

Sir Everard immediately became engrossed with the door of the opposite public-house, to the great discomfiture of one of his gardeners, who was issuing therefrom, slightly inebriated, and had been doing his best to escape the baronet's notice.

Humphrey was delighted with the cigar-cases. They were so brilliant in their embroidered covers. He was particularly attracted by the smallest and smartest.

"It will hold so very few cigars," suggested the woman, "had you not better have a larger one?"

"Oh, that doesn't matter the least," said Humphrey, "because father doesn't smoke. As long as it is smart and pretty to put into his pocket, it will do very well. Wrap it up, please, so as to hide it quite, in case he should guess by the shape."

The widow wrapped it in several covers, and Humphrey left the shop.

"You did not see, father, I hope," he said earnestly, as he mounted his pony, and Sir Everard assured him he had not once looked towards the window.

"How much?" asked the baronet, as the parcel was handed up.

"Ten-and-sixpence," answered the shop-woman.

Sir Everard hid his feelings, and paid the money.

"Isn't it cheap?" said Humphrey, as they rode off, "considering it's all embroidered with gold, and ... oh! dear me! I hope you haven't guessed by that?"

"Far from it," answered Sir Everard; "I am more puzzled than ever; for I can't conceive what you could have found in that little shop, that would be all embroidered with gold."

Humphrey was in great glee. "You haven't the slightest *idea*, I suppose, father what it is?"

"Not the remotest."

"So I know something you don't. You often tell me you know so many things I know nothing about. Now it is just the other way, isn't it?"

"Just the other way," answered the baronet, and Humphrey rode on in a state of great elation.

"It's a dreadful thing to have a secret," he observed presently, after having once or twice begun to speak, and stopped short.

"Why?" inquired his father, smiling.

"Oh! so *dreadfully* difficult to keep," he answered. "Two or three times I've been beginning to talk about it, and forgetting you weren't to know."

"Let's talk of something else then."

Another pause, and then Humphrey said: "Do you know, father, I think you had better take me home?"

"Home already! are you tired?"

"No—it isn't that; but I know if I wait much longer, I shall be telling you the secret before I can stop myself. If I only could tell some one, I should be all right; so that's why I want to get home to Miles."

63

"But I want to call on General Colville and also to pay old Dyson a visit. Can you last a little longer, do you think?"

Humphrey was fond of society, and so took very kindly to the arrangement.

"Dyson is the old deaf man, isn't he? Was he born deaf?"

"No; it is only of late years that he has become so."

"I'm glad I wasn't born deaf. It would have been a great bore. I wonder Dyson doesn't buy an ear-trumpet."

"I suppose, poor fellow, he can't afford it."

"I *should* so like to give him one."

"But where's your money?"

"Ah! there it is again. I never *do* have any money."

"I gave you a shilling a very little while ago."

"I bought copper caps, and hard-bake."

"Ah! we can't eat our cake, and have it, you know."

"Not cake, father—hardbake!"

"It's all the same. Now, if you were to save up your money, instead of buying trash, you would be able to buy useful things."

"So I will. I'll begin saving directly; the very next shilling you give me, I'll put away, and go on till I've got enough to buy Dyson an ear-trumpet."

"That will be a very good plan."

"When do you suppose you'll be giving me another shilling, father?"

"Ah! that I don't know at all."

"Hadn't you better be beginning pretty soon? because an ear-trumpet will cost a good deal, and it would be a pity to keep old Dyson waiting."

Sir Everard handed him a shilling, saying, as he did so: "Now, mind, it is not to be spent on anything else," and Humphrey faithfully promised it should not.

Old Dyson was in his garden when they passed, so they drew up to speak to him He was not so deaf as to be unable to hear Sir Everard's powerful shout, but Humphrey's little attempts were futile.

"How pleased he'd be," thought Humphrey to himself, "if he knew I was going to save up my money to buy him an ear-trumpet."

And he held up his shilling to the old man in triumph, as if the very sight of it would tell him the whole story.

Dyson smiled and nodded. "Ay, ay, going to buy sweeties, I see!"

Humphrey shook his head vehemently, and tried to shout an explanation.

"No!" said the old man; "then it'll be a top, maybe?"

It was no use trying to make him understand; and as Sir Everard was moving off, Humphrey was obliged to follow, shaking his head to the last.

"It would never do to tell old Dyson a secret," he observed to his father, when he overtook him.

"Why not?"

"Why, you'd have to scream it so loud in his ear that every one would hear. It wouldn't be much of a secret when all the village was listening. Supposing I were to shout to him, 'Dyson, I'm going to give father a birthday present, and it's a cigar ca——.' Oh, good gracious!" said Humphrey, pulling up his pony, "I've told you my secret! Oh, father, *did* you guess?"

Sir Everard's attention had been wandering, and he could honestly assure the child that he was as far as ever from knowing the secret.

"And now, here we are at General Colville's," he added; "so you will have lots of things to distract your thoughts."

Sir Everard and Humphrey were shown into the drawing-room where were two ladies and some children.

Mrs. Colville came forward to receive them, and informed Sir Everard that her husband was confined to his room with a slight attack of gout.

Sir Everard immediately volunteered to go and see him. Mrs. Colville took him up-stairs, and Humphrey was left with the other lady.

"What is your name, dear?" she asked.

"I'm Humphrey Duncombe," he answered, seating himself by her side. "Who are you?"

"I'm Mrs. Colville's sister," she answered, smiling. "I suppose you don't remember me, but I have seen you before, at your grandmother's, at Banleigh. I live close by."

"I wonder if you could keep a secret?" said Humphrey eagerly.

"Yes, dear, I think so; but why? Have you got one to tell me?"

"A very great one. I've never had one before, and I don't like it at all. I *must* tell some one, or else I shall be telling it to father, you know."

"But why not tell your father? Surely he would be the best person."

"Tell father! Mrs. Colville's sister? Why, he's just the very person who isn't to know."

"Mrs. Colville's sister" had been half afraid she was going to be made the confidante of some boyish escapade which the child had concealed from his father; but Humphrey's open face disarmed

66

suspicion, and she listened attentively while he poured forth his tale.

It was necessary to listen attentively, for, in the first place, Humphrey was in such a hurry to get to his point, that he rather slurred over the necessary explanations; and, in the second place, he insisted on whispering it all in her ear, on account of the presence of the children.

He had just finished his story, and she was making solemn protestations of the strictest secrecy, when Mrs. Colville came back.

"You must not tell even *her* you know," concluded Humphrey; and, with a sigh of relief, he sat down again.

Mrs. Colville was one of those mothers who are always fancying other children are better dressed than their own. She was a great copyist, and an unscrupulous borrower of patterns.

Virginie held her in abhorrence. She had once asked for the pattern of Miles's blouse, and Virginie had never forgotten or forgiven Sir Everard's ready acquiescence.

Mrs. Colville and her family came to the same church as the Duncombes, and it was almost more than Virginie could stand to see other children dressed like her young gentlemen.

Mrs. Colville—blinded, a little, like most mothers—did not see that what suited Humphrey and Miles, both exceedingly pretty children, did not have quite the same effect on her nice, but decidedly plain, little boys, and went steadily on. Whatever appeared on Humphrey's graceful figure one Sunday, was sure to be reproduced on some fat little Colville the next.

Men do not notice these things. Sir Everard was quite unaware of what went on, but, to Virginie, it was a constant source of annoyance.

"*That's* a pretty suit," said Mrs. Colville examining Humphrey's clothes.

"Very," returned her sister; "they fit so well."

"Come here, Clement," said Mrs. Colville to a little boy in the distance; "there, don't you see, Mary, how differently his things set?"

Mary saw well enough, and saw too that it was figure and not clothes that made such a difference between the two boys, but she did not like to wound her sister's maternal vanity by saying so.

"Does your French bonne make your clothes, dear?" Mrs. Colville inquired of Humphrey.

"Not mine," he answered—"only Miles's. Mine," he added with great pride, "come from a London tailor's."

"Do you happen to remember his name?"

"Swears and Wells," answered Humphrey; "I went there once to see 'Gulliver.' I advise you to go and see him when you are in London. You can't think how jolly he is!"

"I suppose, of course, you don't remember the direction?" Of course Humphrey didn't.

"Stop a bit," he said, all of a sudden. "I've seen the direction written somewhere quite lately. Where *could* I have seen it? Why, since I've been in this room I've read it."

"Impossible, my dear child," said Mrs. Colville, laughing.

"But I have *really*," getting up from his chair in his excitement; "I've seen the number and the name of the street written somewhere in this drawing-room."

"You must be dreaming, dear."

"No, I'm quite sure I did. Now where *could* it have been? Did I go near the writing-table?" As he spoke, he advanced. "Or, stop, here are some cards. Did I see it written on a card?"

"No; I assure you Swears and Wells are not visitors of mine."

Humphrey was determined not to give it up, and in spite of the laughter of both ladies, he got up, went to the door, and made his entry all over again, that he might see what he could have passed on the way that might have had the direction on it.

He reflected out loud as he went along: "I came in here and passed the table (no, not on the books, or the work-basket, or the flower-stand). Then I stood by the piano a minute, while father was shaking hands with Mrs. Colville (no, not on the piano or the music). Then I shook hands with Mrs. Colville, then I sat down on

69

the sofa by her sister, and put my hat by my side so—and——
Oh!" he exclaimed, so suddenly that he startled both ladies, "here
it is, written inside my hat! *That's* where I saw it—look! a little
ticket: 'Swears and Wells, 192 Regent Street.' *Ain't* you glad, Mrs.
Colville? Now you'll be able to find the shop. Hadn't you better
write it down?"

He was heart and soul in the subject, and did not perceive the
amusement he gave.

What would Virginie's feelings have been could she have seen the
name, number and address, copied with great accuracy into Mrs.
Colville's "Where is it?" and to make sure there should be no
mistake, this memorandum added: "a suit such as was lately made
for Sir E. Duncombe's little boy"?

This was just accomplished when Sir Everard came back.

"I'm afraid the General is in for a sharp attack, Mrs. Colville."

"I am afraid he is—he is so very imprudent. You know my sister,
Sir Everard?"

Sir Everard advanced with a smile of recognition.

"Is it possible you are little Mary Wilberforce? I didn't recognize
you just now, you are grown out of all recollection. To be sure, it
is a long time since I saw you—three or four years, isn't it?"

Mary said something about it being a long time, but she did not
like to particularize the date, though she remembered it perfectly:
because Lady Duncombe had been with him at the time, and she
was afraid of recalling painful associations.

"And when did you leave Banleigh?"

"About a week ago."

"How were my people?"

"I saw Lady Albinia and Miss Duncombe the day before I left.
They were both very well."

A shy smile lighted up her face as she mentioned Miss Duncombe. There was evidently some joke about her, for it was reflected on Sir Everard's. "Poor old Cecilia," laughed he.

Miss Duncombe was a lady of limited intellect, and exceedingly young for her age; and everybody was at liberty to laugh at her. They talked on about her for some time, while Humphrey listened with all his might, and then Sir Everard took his leave.

"I'm better now," said Humphrey, as they rode along.

"What! were you not feeling well?" said Sir Everard, alarmed.

"Oh, yes; but I mean about my secret. What makes me feel better is, that I've told it to that lady—Mrs. Colville's sister."

"I don't believe you will ever keep that secret for ten days more. Do you know my birthday is not till Monday week?"

"Oh dear! oh dear! I thought it was much sooner than that. Let's be quick and talk of something else!"

"What shall we talk about? I am expecting two gentlemen down from London to-night, to spend Sunday; and I'm going to meet them at the station, as soon as I have taken you home to your tea. Will that do?"

"Yes, that will do. Are they nice gentlemen?"

"Yes, I think them so: but then tastes differ. Perhaps you won't."

"Old or young?"

"Well! one is a good deal older than me and——"

"White hair, then *of course*?" put in Humphrey.

"Greyish, perhaps; and the other is about the age of your uncle Charlie."

"Will he tell us such nice stories about kangaroos and boar-hunting?"

71

"I should think probably not. The other one is more likely to tell you stories, as he has had little boys of his own."

"Miles and I know of a pond where the branch of a tree hangs over, just like the one in Uncle Charlie's story; and we are going to crawl along it some day, and look down at our faces in the water, like the man did."

"Now, Humphrey," said Sir Everard, "I won't have it done. The branch is quite rotten, and may break off any minute."

Humphrey looked very mournful. "Are you quite sure, father?"

"Quite sure; and I forbid you to do it. Do you hear?"

"Very well, father," with a sigh; "we won't crawl along, if you don't like it; but you won't mind our going to look at it? We've been prevented so many times, and we do so want to go there! If we *promise* not to climb, you won't say we're not to go, *will* you?"

"Yes—once for all, I say you are not to go near the pond; and I trust to you, Humphrey, to obey me. Promise."

"It's a *great* pity, father!"

"Never mind. I won't have Miles led into any more mischief."

Humphrey promised rather reluctantly adding to himself: "It's not much use making *me* promise anything, because I'm *sure* to forget."

They rode on in silence for some time after this; and when Humphrey next spoke, it was on quite a different subject.

"I didn't know till to-day, father, that you didn't like Aunt Cecilia!"

"What *do* you mean, Humphrey?" said Sir Everard, horrified.

"You spoke as if you didn't much like her, to Mrs. Colville's sister."

"Why, what did I say?" said Sir Everard, hastily casting back his thoughts to the conversation.

"Well, you seemed to laugh at her a good deal."

"My dear child," said Sir Everard, relieved, "having a little joke about a person does not prove one does not like that person. I am very fond of your Aunt. It would be odd indeed if I did not like my only sister. Why, when I laugh at you and Miles, do you think I do not like you?"

It was a lame sentence, badly put together, and not expressing much. Sir Everard was not at all satisfied with it himself. He had got it up in such a hurry that he was not at all sure whether it was sense or not, and he was anxious to see if it would answer its purpose. Children are sometimes, however, very easily silenced; and Humphrey received the explanation with great respect.

The danger was past, for this time; but Sir Everard, inwardly resolved never to speak before the children again; and the anxieties of the evening before recurring at the same moment to his mind, he determined not to run any more risks.

So, on arriving at home, he sent up a private message to Virginie that he should not require either of the young gentlemen down-stairs that evening, though they might come to his dressing-room as usual.

Then, after transferring the precious parcel from his own to Humphrey's pocket, he wished the boy "good-bye," and went to meet his friends at the station.

CHAPTER VII.

The next day was Sunday, and a hopelessly wet one. Humphrey and Miles made great friends with their father's guests at breakfast—the former giving them the whole account of the aborigines' dinner-party and the birthday present.

As soon as breakfast was over, Sir Everard and one of his friends went into the library to look for a book they had been talking about, and the two little boys were left with the other gentleman.

Presently Virginie looked in. "M. Humphrey! M. Miles!"

Little Miles jumped up, and went to the door, but Humphrey took no notice.

"Je vous attends, M. Humphrey."

"I'm not coming," said Humphrey. "I'm going to stay and amuse this gentleman."

"Je reviendrai bientôt," said Virginie and she went away, with Miles.

"Is your nurse French?" enquired Colonel Sturt.

"Yes—she's French."

"Then why do you speak to her in English?"

"I never speak French on Sunday," answered Humphrey; "I don't think it's right."

"Not right! Why not?"

"Lessons are wrong on Sunday; and French is a sort of lessons—so French must be wrong too."

"Humphie," said little Miles, running in: "Virginie says you *must* come, or you'll be late for chairs."

"What does he mean?" asked Colonel Sturt.

"He means prayers," answered Humphrey; "he always calls them 'chairs' because he only sees the long rows before we begin, as he's too young to stay. I suppose, as it's so wet, we are not going to church."

"Oh, that's it—is it? Well I'm inclined to think you ought to go then, Humpty-Dumpty, or whatever it is he calls you."

The little boys thought this a capital joke.

"Why, Humpty-Dumpty was the man who sat on a wall!"

"Yes, and had a great fall—which is just what you'll do in a minute," said the Colonel to Humphrey, who had climbed up the back of his chair, and was sitting astride on the top.

"Humpty-Dumpty was an egg," said Humphrey. "*I* don't break so easily. Come along, Miles." And he jumped down and ran off, followed by his brother, both singing:

> "Humpty-Dumpty sat on a wall,
> Humpty-Dumpty had a great fall."

The echoes of their merry voices died away as they ran up-stairs, and the concluding words were not distinguishable.

Five minutes after, the gong sounded, and the servants filed into the library.

Humphrey was in his place by his father, Mr. Wemyss seated near, and everything ready. But Colonel Sturt had not appeared. Humphrey looked up anxiously at every sound.

Sir Everard concluded he did not mean to come, so he opened his book, and signed to one of the servants to shut the door. Humphrey's restless eyes followed his friend William's movements as he rose to obey. The next moment he was convulsed with laughter, and could scarcely restrain himself.

No one else seemed to see anything amusing, and Sir Everard began to read with his usual gravity; but Humphrey, though he got better as the service proceeded, did not dare glance towards the servants' end of the room, and had to keep his eyes fixed on his prayer-book, for fear they should be tempted to stray in that direction. What was it that had tickled the boy's fancy?

Only that just as William was closing the door, the missing gentleman had slipped quietly in and unconsciously seated himself in the footman's vacant place at the end of the long line of servants, where he remained during the rest of the service.

The sight of him there, combined with the expression of William's face at finding his place occupied, had at first completely upset Humphrey; but, after a time, the veneration for solemn things, which was so prominent a feature in his character, came to his help and he became engrossed in his responses.

The afternoon proving as wet as the morning, Sir Everard, for want of something better to do, showed his friends over the house. He had a few good pictures, and the ceiling of one of the upper rooms; was curiously painted; otherwise there was, not much to see.

Wandering about a thinly-inhabited house on a wet day is always rather depressing and it would have been a melancholy business, but for the children. But Humphrey and Miles chased each other along the passages, and made the unoccupied rooms ring with their merry voices. They were very anxious to do the honors of their own apartments, when, in due course, the nurseries were reached.

"This is my bed," proclaimed Humphrey and "Here is my bath," announced Miles.

"But what's this?" said Colonel Sturt, taking up an embroidered cigar-case that lay upon the table.

A shriek was the only answer.

Colonel Sturt nearly dropped the cigar-case in his consternation; Sir Everard turned hastily round; and Humphrey, snatching it up, rushed out of the room.

"What is the matter?" asked Sir Everard.

"*It was the birthday present!*" said little Miles, in an awe-struck whisper.

Sir Everard followed Humphrey to assure him he had not seen anything; which made matters rather worse, as he found him in the act of hiding it in Virginie's band-box, under her best Sunday bonnet. With some difficulty he reassured the boy, and brought him back.

"It was a near thing, though," observed Humphrey, with a sigh of relief.

Colonel Sturt was now almost afraid to remark on anything else; but a shilling concealed in a tooth-glass attracted his attention.

"Oh, that's my money," explained Humphrey, "that I am saving to buy old Dyson an ear-trumpet with. It was the only safe place I could find to keep it in."

"How much will it cost?" asked the Colonel.

"Seventeen shillings, I believe."

"And how much have you got?"

"Well, only that yet," answered the boy, pointing to the solitary shilling; "but then you know, I only began yesterday."

Colonel Sturt asked a good many questions about old Dyson, and then took half-a-sovereign from his pocket, and dropped it into the tooth-glass. "That's my contribution," said he.

Humphrey was too much excited by this unexpected munificence to make civil speeches; but his unfeigned surprise and delight were worth all the thanks in the world. He ran after his father to exhibit his treasure, and returned breathless.

"Only think!" he said to Colonel Sturt, "that other gentlemen has given me six shillings; so now I can buy the trumpet directly, and I thought it would be weeks and weeks before I got it!"

The children were now summoned to their tea, and told to wish the gentlemen "good-night," as they were not to come down to dinner.

But Humphrey first extorted a promise from Colonel Sturt, that he would go to the ear-trumpet shop the next day, the very minute he arrived in London, and have it sent off directly.

Sir Everard had nearly finished dressing that evening, when the door was thrown open, and both boys rushed into the room.

"There! take it father," said Humphrey holding out the cigar-case—"that's for you. That's your birthday present—the grand secret! It's no use our trying to keep it any longer, because we *can't!*"

"Are you surprised, Fardie?" asked little Miles, clapping his hands, and Humphrey eagerly repeated the question.

Sir Everard could, with all truth, assure the children that he had never been so surprised in his life; for, as he did not smoke, certainly the very last present he would have expected was a cigar-case!

But his pleasure and gratitude were so well feigned, that the children went to bed highly delighted with the success of their birthday present.

─────────

CHAPTER VIII.

"Good-bye, Humpty-Dumpty! The trumpet shall be at the station at five o'clock this afternoon without fail."

So spoke Colonel Sturt, as Sir Everard drove his two friends from the door the next morning.

Humphrey waved his hat in answer, and flew off to make arrangements with Virginie for going to the station to meet it. He had his father's leave for himself and Miles to go there with the coachman, and to be dropped afterwards at old Dyson's, where Virginie was to meet them, and bring them home.

Nothing could be more perfect! At about half-past four, the dog-cart drove up to the door, and off they went, followed by many parting injunctions from Virginie as to getting in and out carefully, and sitting very still.

The trumpet was waiting at the station, and was safely delivered into their eager hands.

On the way to old Dyson's, Humphrey opened the parcel, and displayed the ear-trumpet to Miles.

Never had they seen so curious an article! It was composed of three tubes, each fitting into the next, and it lengthened or shortened at will.

Humphrey got very impatient to arrive, and tried to persuade the coachman to whip up the horse into a gallop; but steady old Peter didn't see it at all.

Humphrey then amused himself by lengthening out the tubes, and trumpeting loudly through them; causing the horse to start so violently, that little Miles was almost pitched out. Then, in shutting it up again, he dropped it into the road, and they had to wait while he got out and picked it up.

All this causing a delay, Peter was told on arriving at the cottage, that Virginie had already been there, but that, finding she was too soon, she had walked on to the village, and was to call again in a few minutes.

This information he gathered from a woman who was standing at the gate, and who assisted the children to alight.

Then, having deposited them safely, Peter drove off; and Humphrey, brandishing his trumpet, rushed down the little garden, and beat a thundering tattoo on old Dyson's door. But, loud as it was, it did not make any impression on the deaf old man, who was sitting in his arm-chair, indulging in an afternoon nap.

One minute Humphrey waited, and then his patience gave way. He raised the latch, and the two children entered the cottage.

"He's asleep," whispered Miles.

"You must go and give him a little shake," said Humphrey.

Miles advanced timidly. He didn't much like the job, but disobedience to Humphrey was a thing he never dreamt of.

Humphrey hid the trumpet behind him, and waited eagerly.

Miles's gentle shake produced no effect at all; Dyson only smiled pleasantly in his sleep.

"Shake his hand," said Humphrey.

Miles looked doubtfully at the horny hand lying on the arm of the chair, and flushed a little as he put his tiny fingers upon it. But the old man did not move.

"Harder!" cried Humphrey.

Miles exerted himself to the utmost, and succeeded better, for the old man turned over to one side of his chair, and lifted his head a little.

Miles retreated a few steps. But it was a false alarm, for old Dyson's head fell forward again.

"You must jump on his knee, Miles."

The pretty little face lengthened considerably.

"Oh, Humphie! must I really?"

"Why not?"

"Don't much like it, Humphie."

"What! afraid of poor old Dyson! Never mind, I'll do it."

And, putting the trumpet on the floor, Humphrey sprang upon the old man, and shook him so vigorously that he woke in a fright; but when he saw his little visitors, he sat down again with a smile, saying, "Aye, aye, Mamselle said I was to expect you; and how are ye to-day, my pretty dears?"

"Quite well, thank you," said Miles, drawing nearer.

Dyson put his hand behind his ear: "I don't hear what you say," he said, rather sadly; "I'm an old man, and I'm getting deafer every day."

Humphrey chuckled with delight, and Miles looked up smiling.

"He'll hear soon, won't he, Humphie?"

"Dyson!" shouted Humphrey, backing a few steps and beckoning, "come here."

The unsuspecting old man rose and advanced. The boy was watching his opportunity, and directly he was near enough Humphrey snatched up the trumpet, and putting it up, shouted such a "How are you?" into the old man's ear, that the shock caused Dyson to bound into the air, and then fall backwards with such force, that if he had not providentially fallen into his chair, he might never have survived to tell the tale. And there he remained, sputtering and panting, shaking his head about, as if he felt he would never get rid of the vibration.

The two little boys stood aghast. As good luck would have it, the woman who had met them at the gate was of an inquisitive disposition; and wondering what was going on in the cottage, she had for some time been peeping in at the window.

She understood at once the position of affairs, and came hastily in.

Raising the old man from his chair, she explained to him what had happened. It was some minutes before he understood, for he was bewildered and alarmed: but he took it in at last, and the children had the satisfaction of receiving his thanks, and assurances that he was by no means ungrateful for their present.

Then the woman spoke gently to him through the trumpet, and his look of pleasure at hearing so clearly, and his "Well! to be sure!" was a great delight to the two little boys.

When Dyson had got accustomed to the sound, he declared himself willing for Humphrey to try again, but the woman suggested that Miles's voice was the softest, to which Humphrey agreed.

Miles took up the trumpet, and his gentle "I'm so sorry Humphie made you jump," was whispered so quietly, that Dyson only just caught the sound.

Then the old man held it out to Humphrey, who, not expecting it, had not got anything to say. So no sooner had he put his lips to it than he went off into such fits of laughter, that Dyson hastily removed the trumpet, and began to rub his ear, "Aye, but it does tickle so." This made Humphrey laugh more, and the woman advised his abandoning the attempt for that day.

By this time, however, Dyson had got so pleased with his new accomplishment, that he declared it his intention to go and pay some visits in the village, saying it was several years since he had had a good chat with his neighbors.

But they all went, the old man hurrying on at a great rate, so eager was he to show off his newly-recovered powers.

The first person they met was Virginie, and Dyson said he must have a word with "Mamselle."

Humphrey was in an excited state, ready for anything; so while Virginie was talking, he called Miles, and told him he thought it would be a capital evening for the pond where the water-lilies grew. There was a stile at the side of the road, which he knew to be a short cut to the pond, and he had no doubt they would be able to find their way.

No recollection of his promise to his father troubled his conscience; and as they were not going to climb the tree, even Virginie could not object!

So he helped his little brother over the stile, and then they both ran with all their might.

Meanwhile Virginie, talking affably through the trumpet, in the high road, did not notice that they had disappeared.

CHAPTER IX.

There was an unusual stir in the quiet household of Wareham Abbey that evening; for at nearly eight o'clock the two little boys had not returned home.

Virginie had not been very much concerned at their absence during the first few hours, as they very often ran on before her, and then betook themselves to some of their favorite haunts.

But when tea-time came and passed, she got uneasy, and went to look for them. Her uneasiness changed to alarm when she had visited in vain the dairy, laundry, swing, gardens, and dog-kennel. Then, when it came on to rain, her anxiety increased; and when from drizzling it changed to a steady down-pour her "nerves" gave way completely, and she returned home to consult with the other servants as to what steps had best be taken.

She went into the housekeeper's room, wringing her hands, and prognosticating all sorts of evils to Miles. "Never, never, would he recover from the effects of such a wetting!"

The gardener was dispatched one way and the coachman another, bearing umbrellas and galoshes.

The two little culprits were soon discovered sitting in a damp ditch, sheltering themselves under a hedge.

Humphrey took great credit to himself for having hit upon this plan.

"The fact was," he said, "the pond and the water-lilies had been so engrossing, that he had forgotten all about the time till he saw the sun beginning to sink; then starting off in a great hurry, they had taken the wrong turning out of the field, and lost their way in the wood."

They were wandering on in the wrong direction, when they met a boy, who had pointed out their mistake, and brought them back to the high road. Here Humphrey had suddenly recollected that rain was apt to give his little brother cold, and with great pride in his own forethought had established him, dripping wet as he already was, under the hedge where they had been sitting for about half an hour before the coachman found them.

It was no use Virginie venting her wrath upon Humphrey. All that could be done now, was to get Miles into bed as quickly as could be, and ward off ill effects if possible.

But the mischief was done. Miles tossed about all night, and woke next morning with an oppression on his chest, which was always with him the forerunner of an attack on the lungs.

The doctor came to see him, and ordered him to be kept in bed.

Humphrey spent the morning with his little brother, but was dismissed at last, as talking only made Miles cough.

In the afternoon Miles got worse, and Virginie sent off again for the doctor.

Humphrey kept out of her way, feeling that he was in disgrace, and went out into the garden. He felt dull and solitary without his little brother, but, childlike, he had not begun to be anxious, for Miles had often been ill before, and had always got well again. Still there was no fun in anything without him, no exploit any satisfaction without his applause. Humphrey betook himself at last to the little gardens, where he had a friend in the person of Dolly, the laundry-maid. The gardens were close to the laundry, and often, when she was ironing at the window, Dolly had watched the children at their play, and overheard their long conversations. She was perhaps the only person who had seen Humphrey in his serious moods. Unknown to him, she had witnessed one of his rare bursts of feeling at the time of his mother's death, and after that, had ever been one of his staunchest supporters. She could never forget how the little fellow had sobbed over the mustard and cress he had sown for his mother and which had come up too late!

The weather had been dry for some time previously, and it had shown no sign of coming up. Every day he had visited it, that he might cut it for her to eat with her afternoon tea; but every visit had been in vain. Then, on that sad day, when the funeral train had borne away all that remained of her, he had come to his garden in his restless longing to escape from his sorrow, and the first thing that had met his eye was the green A. D. mocking him with its freshness and luxuriance.

"It's no use now," Dolly had heard him sob; "I wish it had never come up!"

This was the very day he had been chasing the young lambs in the meadow, while his father watched him from the window and this was how it had ended.

Humphrey found a good deal to do in his garden, and worked away busily for some time; he then assisted Dolly to turn the mangle, and bottled some soap-suds for future bubble blowing. He also informed her of the honor in store for her at the Harvest Home, and anxiously asked her what gown she meant to wear on the occasion. She must be very smart, he said, *awfully* smart! Dolly confided her intention of investing in a new print dress, and consulted him as to the color.

Casting his thoughts back to the smartest thing he had lately seen, they reverted to the cigar-case, and he suggested crimson and gold.

Dolly looked rather scared, and expressed her doubts as to the probability of those colors being found in any print sold in the village.

"Yellow would *do*, you know," said Humphrey, "and it would be like the corn."

So Dolly promised to try and procure a yellow print, with a red stripe or spot; and, if that were impossible, a plain yellow one could no doubt be found.

Time slipped by very quickly, but still Humphrey rather wondered at last that no one should call him in to his tea; and after a while he put his tools away, and wished Dolly good-bye.

He gathered a few young radishes for a treat for Miles, and then ran home.

He was surprised to find the nursery door locked, and began to kick it.

"Miles!" he called out, "I've brought you some radishes. Ouvrez, Virginie, c'est moi!"

The door was opened with an angry jerk, and Virginie flounced into the passage.

Humphrey saw at a glance that she was in one of what he and Miles called "her states," but whether it was of anger or alarm, he could not at first make out. It was always a bad sign when her face was enveloped in flannel, as was now the case. Virginie always tied up her face on the smallest provocation, though to what end the children had never discovered. But anyhow, she was sure to be out of temper when she did so, and Humphrey waited rather anxiously to hear what she had to say.

She burst into a voluble flow of talk, which, owing to her excitement, the boy found it difficult to follow. He managed however, to gather that Miles was very, very ill, that the doctor was very much alarmed about him; that it was all his (Humphrey's) fault; that he had woke Miles by kicking at the door just as she had hoped he was going to get some sleep; that he was to go away and keep away, and that everybody, including the doctor, was very angry with him.

Then she retreated into the room, and shut the door, leaving him standing in the passage, with his bunch of radishes in his hand.

All the light faded out of Humphrey's face, as he tried to think over what he had just heard.

"Miles so ill that the doctor was frightened."

That was the most prominent idea at first, and in his dread and apprehension, Humphrey hardly dared move.

Sometimes he put his eye to the keyhole, to see if he could discover what was going on in the room, and then, lying down on the door-mat, he listened with all his might.

The silence within, only broken by whispering voices, frightened him, and his heart began to beat loudly.

If only the child could have looked into the room and seen his little brother lying in bed half asleep, and Virginie putting a linseed poultice on his chest, or whispering to Jane to bring her his cooling-draught, his fears would have vanished.

But it is ever so with sudden illness. Those who are kept in the dark always have the worst of it; for mystery and suspense are, like anticipation, always worse than reality. Imagination runs riot, and brings great suffering to the outsiders. How much are children to be pitied on these occasions! Everyone's thoughts are necessarily with the invalid, and no one has time to bestow a word on the poor little trembling things standing outside the sick-room. They feel they are useless, and considered in the way; and do not dare make inquiries of the maids who run in and out of the room—with important faces, who probably could not stop to answer even if they did; and so are left to magnify every sound into some terrible significance, which probably has no foundation but in their own disordered fancies.

There is terror in whispering voices, agony in the sharp ringing of a bell, mystery even in the calling for spoons and glasses, and their jingling as they are handed in.

All this, and more, was experienced by little Humphrey Duncombe. I say *more*, because his fears were not those of ordinary children. The dread I have been describing is for the most part a nameless dread; the children know not why they fear, nor what; it is all vague and undefined, because they have no experience of sorrow.

But remember that this child was no stranger to sickness and death; that into his little life they had already entered; that the grim visitor had swept through the walls of his home, and left it very empty. What had happened once, might happen again. So he gave it all up at once, "Miles was dying! perhaps already dead!"

A child of Humphrey's disposition suffers intensely when face to face with sorrow. Granted that the power of being easily distracted is a mitigation, it does not alter the feeling *for the time*. Life, past and future, is grafted into the misery of the present, and existence itself is a blank.

He was so tender-hearted, too, poor little fellow! so remorseful for his errors, so sensitive to an unkind word. Yet, as we have seen, with all this, he was so heedless, thoughtless, and volatile, that no one could give him credit for any depth of feeling; and even his father (though he would not have had it otherwise, though he rejoiced that he should have the capability of turning into enjoyment, both for himself and Miles every event of their lonely child-life) had marvelled at him, and had more than once said to himself, "The boy has no heart!"

No heart! why, as we see him there in the passage, his poor little heart is filled to bursting.

Stung by Virginie's harsh words, wrung with fear for his little brother, alarmed as much for his father's grief as his father's anger, and remorseful at the thought of his own broken promise, Humphrey sank down on the ground, and cried as if his heart would break.

In addition to the grief, it was such a dreadful feeling, that, in a trouble like this, no one cared to help him; that he was looked upon as the cause of it all; that his hand seemed against every man, and every man's hand against him.

His sorrow must be greater than theirs, he reflected. Was not Miles more to him than to Virginie? And yet they left him— sobbing and crying—unheeded.

Lying there, crouched up by the door such an awful sense of loneliness came down upon the boy's soul. In the hour of his trouble he needed pity so much, and no one gave it to him.

Then there arose in his heart such a terrible longing for his mother; such a yearning, that would not be quieted, for all that he had had, and all that he had lost; such an overwhelming sense of the void in his life, that he could not bear it, and he started to his feet with a sob which was almost a cry.

This feeling *must* go, he could not bear it, and he fought with it with desperation; for it was an old enemy, one with whom he had often wrestled in desperate conflict before, and upon whose attacks he always looked back with horror. Deep down in his heart it had its being, but it was only every now and then that it rose up to trouble him.

Of late it had assailed him much less, its attacks had been weaker, and occurring at much longer intervals. Why has it risen with such relentless force now? How is he to resist it? How is he to fight with it? This blank, empty feeling, how is he to drive it away?

He tried to think of his garden, of his games, and of all the things which constituted the joy of his young existence.

Children of a larger growth, but children in understanding still, do not many of us wrestle with this undefined feeling in the same way? This mysterious thing, which we, with our maturer experience, call sorrow, is not our first thought when it assails us, "How shall we drive it away?" Call it grief, despair, disappointment, anxiety, care—call it what you will, do we not try to drown it in change of thought of some kind? Does it not drive the rich to society, traveling, or excitement, and the poor to the public-house?

Here were the passages where he had romped with Miles; here were the stairs down which he had jumped that very morning, and the balustrades down which he had slid; why did they look so different?

God help him! the emptiness in his heart was so great, that it was repeating itself on all around. There was no help to be got from the feeling of his recent happiness in the old house. Never had it seemed so dreary; never had he realized before what an empty house it was, occupied only in one corner by a nurse and two little boys.

There was no sound, no life anywhere; the twilight was creeping over the silent hall and staircase, and he knew it was deepening in the uninhabited rooms below. And then, as if to mock him with the contrast, came before him so vivid a recollection of life with his mother in the house; of her voice and her laugh upon that staircase; of her presence in those rooms; so clear and distinct a vision of her soft eyes and gentle smile, that the motherless child could bear it no longer, and covering his face with his hands to shut out the sight of the emptiness, he fled away down the passage, as if he thought to leave the desolation behind.

But the emptiness was with him as he went; all down the stairs and through the hall it pursued him; it gained upon him as he stood with his hand upon the drawing-room door; it preceded him into the darkened room, and was waiting for him when he entered.

The light that came in through the chinks of the shutters was very faint, but his longing eye sought the picture, and he could just distinguish the sweet face and the smiling babe in her arms.

He ran forward, and threw himself on the sofa beneath it.

"Mother!" he sobbed, "I want you back so much! Every one is angry with me, and I am so very miserable!"

Cold, blank silence all around; mother and child smiled on, unconscious of his words; even as he gazed the light faded away from the picture, and he was left alone in the gathering darkness!

In vain he tried to fancy himself once more the child in the picture; in vain he tried to fancy he felt her arms around him, and her shoulder against his head. It would not do! In fits of passion or disobedience he had come here, and the memory of his mother had soothed him, and sent him away penitent; but in this dreadful sense of loneliness he wanted comfort, and of comfort he found none.

*   *   *   *   *

Yet was there comfort near, if he would but ask for it, and of the very kind he wanted: "As one whom his mother comforteth, so will I comfort you." He knew it not; he cried not for it. He was not ignorant of God's omnipresence; in ordinary times the boy believed with a child's simple faith that God was always near him, but in the hour of his trouble he was incapable of deriving any comfort from the knowledge, incapable of any thought but his own sorrow.

Children of a larger growth, but children in understanding still, do not many of us, in spite of our maturer experience, do likewise? "There is no help," we say; "our trouble is greater than we can bear." We lie like the child, crushed and despairing, and God, who at other times we feel to be so near, seems hidden from us altogether.

But thank God it is only *seems*, not *is*. He is unchangeable, and unaffected by our changeability. Hidden, it may be, by the cloud we have ourselves raised, the dark cloud of hopelessness, He is still there, the Same whose presence we realise so fully in happier moments. "He," says a writer of the present century, "is immutable, unchangeable, while we are different every hour. What He is in Himself, the great unalterable I Am, not what we in this or that moment feel Him to be, *that* is our hope."

The comfort, then, for us and for the stricken child is, that though we may not at such times do our part, He is ever ready to do His; and it would almost seem as if He were providing for this state of feeling when he says, "*Before* they call, I will answer." But what *could* be done for the child in the terrible hour of his trouble? *We* know not, but God knew. The little heart was open before Him, and He knew that his sorrow would flee at morning light, and that he only wanted comfort for the present moment. So, looking pityingly down upon the lonely child, He sent him the only thing that could help him—laid gently upon his heavy eyelids the only

92

gift that could do him any good—giving him the peace of unconsciousness till the hour of sorrow and sighing should pass away!

There one of the maids found him an hour or so later, and carried him up to bed without waking him.

CHAPTER X.

Humphrey slept late the next morning, and the sun was streaming on his face when he awoke.

He sprang out of bed with an exclamation of delight at seeing such a fine day, and then started back in surprise at finding himself in a strange room.

Recollections of last night were beginning to steal over him, when the door opened, and Jane came in.

"At last! Master Humphrey. Why I thought you were never going to wake up! Master Miles has been asking for you for ever so long!"

"Then he's better, is he?" said Humphrey, eagerly.

"Better!" exclaimed Jane, in a sprightly tone; "why bless you, he's quite well."

Jane had been the one to find Humphrey in the drawing-room the night before, and had guessed by his tear-stained face how it had been.

She was not equivocating; Miles had taken a turn for the better in the night, and there was no further anxiety about him.

Humphrey's spirits rose immediately to their usual height; he dressed himself in a great hurry, and soon the two little brothers were together again.

Humphrey did not allude to his troubles of the evening before. Perhaps he had already forgotten them; or if they did recur to his memory, it was with a dull, dead sense of pain which he had no wish to call into life again.

His was a nature that was only too glad to escape from such recollections. His buoyant spirits and volatile disposition helped him to throw off sad memories, and never had he been gayer or wilder than on this morning, as he laughed and talked, and played by his brother's bedside.

It was a glorious day, Miles was nearly well, his father was coming (in obedience to Virginie's letter), and life seemed to him one flood of sunshine.

Virginie, however, still shaky from her late anxiety, and with her head ominously tied up with flannel, looked grimly on his mirth. She did not understand the boy: how should she? She was feeling very sore with him for having caused all this trouble; she was, of course, ignorant of what he had suffered, and she looked upon his noisy merriment as only another proof of his usual heartlessness.

Humphrey was not in the room when his father arrived, having gone out for a run in the garden; so Virginie had no check in pouring out her complaint.

Sir Everard was startled at the effect the short illness had had upon Miles, and listened more patiently than usual.

The delicate child looked so much like his mother as he lay in bed, with his flushed cheeks and lustrous eyes, that the vague fear about him, that almost always haunted the father, took a more definite shape.

Certainly Virginie's account of Humphrey's disobedience was not calculated to soften him towards the boy, and he really felt more angry with him than he had ever done before.

Little Miles was particularly engaging that day, so delighted to see his father, and so caressing in his ways, that Humphrey's want of heart seemed to stand out in sharper contrast. Sir Everard could not tear himself away from the little fellow for some time, and the more coaxing the child was, the more painfully came home to the father the thought of having so nearly lost him.

On descending from the nursery, Sir Everard went into the library, and ringing the bell, desired that Master Duncombe should be sent to him immediately.

"I don't suppose I shall make any impression upon him," he said to himself while he waited, "but I must try." He never expected much of Humphrey, but he was hardly prepared for the boisterous opening of the door, and the gay aspect of the boy as he bounded into the room.

Sir Everard was, as we have seen, always loth to scold or punish either of his motherless children, and when it must be done, he schooled himself to do it from a sense of duty. But the bold, and, as it seemed to him, defiant way in which the boy presented himself, fairly angered him, and it was in a tone of no forced displeasure that he exclaimed, "What do you mean, sir, by coming into the room like that?"

Now Humphrey had been busy working in his garden when his father's message had reached him, in happy forgetfulness of his recent conduct and his brother's recent danger.

In the excitement of hearing of his father's arrival, he had overlooked the probability of his displeasure; and it was with unfeigned astonishment that he heard himself thus greeted. His wondering expression only irritated his father the more.

"Don't stand there, looking as if you thought you had done nothing wrong," he exclaimed testily; "do you think you are to lead your poor little brother into danger, and make him ill, and then not to be found fault with? Don't you know that you have disobeyed me, and broken your promise? Did I not forbid you to go near that pond? I tell you I won't have it, and you shall go to school if you can't behave better at home. Do you hear me, sir? what do you mean by behaving in this way?"

Humphrey understood now. His lips quivered, and his cheek flushed at hearing himself so sternly spoken to, and he dared not attempt to answer, lest he should disgrace himself by tears.

Sir Everard's anger soon evaporated.

"You see, Humphrey," he went on more gently, "it is always the same thing. Day after day and week after week I have the same complaints of you. I should have thought you were old enough

96

now to remember that Miles is very delicate, and that you would have taken care of him, instead of leading him into mischief. Do you know," he concluded, suddenly dropping his voice, "that we have very nearly lost your little brother?"

To Sir Everard's surprise, Humphrey burst into a passion of tears. The words brought back to him the suffering of last night with a sharp pang, and his whole frame shook with sobs.

Sir Everard was instantly melted. Like most men, the sight of tears had a magical effect upon him; and he took the child on his knee, and tried to comfort him.

"There, there," he said soothingly, as he stroked the curly head, "that will do; I must not expect old heads on young shoulders; but you must try and remember what I tell you, and not disobey me any more. And now give me a kiss, and run out, and have a game of cricket."

Humphrey lifted up his tear-stained face and gladly received the kiss of forgiveness.

A few minutes after he was playing single wicket in the field with the footman, without a trace of sorrow on his countenance or a sad thought in his heart.

But Sir Everard remained in the library, perturbed and uneasy. Miles's fragile appearance had made him nervous, and he was thinking how easily any little chill might bring on inflammation again. He was well versed in all the sudden relapses and as sudden improvements of delicate lungs. Had he not watched them hour by hour? Did he not know every step? It was an attack like this that had preceded his wife's slow fading. Daily had he watched the flush deepen and the features sharpen on a face which was so like the little face up-stairs, that, as he thought of them both, he could hardly separate the two.

Something must be done to prevent the recurrence of any risks for Miles. But what? It was clear that Humphrey was not to be trusted; and yet Sir Everard could not bear to spoil the children's fun by separating them, or by letting Virginie mount in too strict guard over them. She was a nervous woman, and too apt to think everything they did had danger in it.

"Boys must amuse themselves," he reflected; "and at Humphrey's age it is natural they should do extraordinary things. I don't want to make him a muff." Involuntarily he smiled at the idea of Humphrey being a muff. "How easily Miles might have fallen into that horrid pond! The slightest push from Humphrey, who never looks where he is going, would have sent him in. Would he ever have recovered the effects of a wholesale soaking? However," he concluded, half out loud, as he rose to return to the nursery, "the session is nearly over, and I shall be down here, and able to look after them myself. And meanwhile I shall remain on for a day or two, till Miles is quite well again."

CHAPTER XI.

It was a pleasant little holiday that Sir Everard spent with his children during the days that followed; and often in after years did he look back upon it with a tender regret.

Miles's health improved steadily, and in a little while he was allowed to be carried in the afternoon to his father's dressing-room where, nestled in a huge arm-chair, with his father and Humphrey sitting by, he passed some very happy hours. Sometimes they played games, or else Sir Everard would read out loud from a book of fairy tales he had brought from London. One evening he read a story which greatly delighted both little boys. It was about a wonderful mirror, which had the power of showing to its owner what any of his absent friends might be doing at the moment he was looking into it.

"Oh, how I *wish* I could have such a mirror!" said Humphrey, very earnestly.

"How I wish I could!" echoed Miles.

"Do you?" said Sir Everard; "I wonder why."

Humphrey did not answer; he was gazing out of the window in deep thought.

"Who would you look for, my little man?" asked Sir Everard of Miles.

"I should look for you, dear Fardie."

"But I am here, darling."

"Not always," said Miles, laying his little hand caressingly on Sir Everard's. "When you are away in London, I should like to look in and see what you are doing."

It was by these engaging little words and ways, that Miles had wound himself so closely round his father's heart.

"So you would like to see me when I am away," he said, stroking the child's hand, "do you miss me when I'm not with you?"

"So much, Fardie; I wish you would never go. Humphie, don't we miss Fardie dreadfully when he's away, and wish he would never go?"

Sir Everard glanced at his elder boy, as if hoping to hear him confirm his little brother's words, but Humphrey was still looking thoughtfully up, out of the window, and took no notice.

"What is he thinking about?" whispered Sir Everard to Miles.

"I don't know," said Miles, softly; "perhaps he's wishing very hard for a mirror."

Whatever the boy was wishing for, it must have been something which he felt he could never have, for the brown eyes were full of tears as they gazed up into the blue sky.

"Wait a minute," breathed Miles, "he'll say how we miss you, when he's done thinking; often, when he's thinking, he doesn't answer me till he's quite done what he's thinking about."

With the tears still standing in them, the eyes suddenly sparkled with a new feeling, and Humphrey sprang to the window, exclaiming,—

"A hawk! I do declare; and he'll have the sparrow in a minute!"

Sir Everard looked disappointed, and drew Miles closer to him.

"He's not thinking about us, is he, darling?"

"Eh!" exclaimed Humphrey, starting, "were you speaking to me? What did you say, Miles?"

"It was about the glass, Humphie; I said we should like so much to see what Fardie is doing in London sometimes."

"Oh, wouldn't it be fun!" said Humphrey, seating himself by his brother; "sometimes we should see him in his club, and sometimes in a Hansom cab, and sometimes we should see you making a speech in the House of Parliament, shouldn't we, father, with your arm out, and a great sheet all round you, like the statue of Mr. Pitt down-stairs?"

Sir Everard laughed.

"Not very often," I think.

"How should we see you, Fardie?"

"I'm afraid, if you looked late in the evening, you would often see me *so*," he answered, folding his arms, and shutting his eyes.

"What, asleep!" exclaimed the children.

"Fast asleep," returned their father.

"Isn't the Queen very angry with you?" inquired Miles.

"The Queen is generally asleep herself at such hours."

"What! in the House of Parliament?"

"No; but in one or other of her palaces."

"But she isn't always asleep at night," said Humphrey, in a superior tone; "sometimes she sits up very late, and has a ball. I know a picture of her giving a ball, in the old book of prints down-stairs."

The volume in question bore the date of 1710, and the engraving represented the court of Queen Anne, but it was all the same to Humphrey.

"Do you ever go to the Queen's ball Fardie?" inquired Miles.

"Yes, dear, I have been, but not for a long time."

"Father's too old for balls now," observed Humphrey. "Ain't you, father?"

"My dancing days are over, yes," said Sir Everard, absently. He was thinking how lovely his wife had looked at the last court ball he had been to.

"Do they dance 'Up the middle and down again,' Fardie?"

"No," answered Sir Everard, smiling, "quadrilles and valses mostly."

"I suppose when you were young and went to balls, they used to dance the minuet?" said Humphrey. "Used you to wear a pig-tail, father?"

"Upon my word!" said Sir Everard, "why, how old do you think I am?"

The children had no idea, and amused themselves for the next ten minutes by trying to guess, their conjectures varying between sixty and ninety.

"Will you come for a run, father?" said Humphrey, presently.

"It's a little hot for running, isn't it?" answered Sir Everard; "but if you are tired of being indoors, you can go in the garden, and I will join you in about an hour."

"We might go to the village, mightn't we, and spend my pennies? Dyson's got his trumpet, so there's nothing to save for, and I should like to spend them."

"Very well: where shall I find you?"

"I shall be feeding my jackdaw, or working in my garden; or, perhaps," after a moment's reflection, "I might be sitting at the top of the apple tree, or running along the kitchen garden wall. But if you don't find me in any of those places, look in the hen-house. I might be getting an egg there for Miles' tea."

"But isn't the hen-house kept locked?"

"Oh, yes, but that doesn't matter a bit. I always squeeze myself through the hen's little trap door."

"You don't expect me to do the same, I hope?"

Humphrey's sense of the ridiculous was tickled by the idea of his father's tall form struggling through the little hole of a few inches wide; and his merry laugh echoed through the room.

"What fun it would be!" he exclaimed, "you'd stick in the middle, and not be able to get in or out. How you would kick!"

Little Miles laughed till he coughed, and Sir Everard was obliged to dismiss Humphrey to the garden.

Humphrey was not engaged in any of the employments he had mentioned when his father joined him an hour later. He was standing gazing thoughtfully at the lame jackdaw hopping about on his wooden leg.

"What a funny boy you are," said his father, laying a hand on his shoulder. "I do believe you care more for that ugly old jackdaw than for anything else that you have. He always seems to me the most uninteresting of creatures and I'm sure he is very ungrateful, for the kinder you are to him the crosser he gets."

"Yes, he's very cross, poor old fellow!" said Humphrey. "Look!" holding out his hand, which bore unmistakable evidence of a bird's beak, "how he's pecked me. He always does whenever I feed him."

"I should almost be inclined not to feed him then."

"I couldn't let him starve, you know. Besides, I don't wonder he's cross. It's enough to make any one angry to be always hopping about in one little place, instead of having the whole world to fly about in. And if it wasn't for me," he added, half to himself, "he would be flying about now."

Sir Everard did not catch the last words, but the boy's face reminded him that he had touched on a painful subject, and he hastened to change it by proposing they should start for the village.

Humphrey brightened up directly, and was soon talking as gaily as usual. The painfulness of the subject consisted in this.

One day, Humphrey and Miles were amusing themselves in their gardens, when the jackdaw, then young and active, came flying past.

Humphrey without the slightest idea of touching it, flung a stone at it, exclaiming, "Get away, old fellow!"

But so unerring was his aim, that the stone struck the bird on the wing, and brought it struggling and fluttering to the ground.

Dolly, the laundry-maid, was close at hand, and she never forgot Humphrey's burst of grief and remorse, when, on picking up the jackdaw, they found both leg and wing broken. That a living creature should be deprived of its powers by his means was more than the tender-hearted child could bear, and for a long while he was inconsolable.

In due time the bird had been supplied with a wooden leg through Dolly, by whom it had ever since been carefully tended, but its life, in Humphrey's eyes, was over; and he never passed the cage without a pang. He seldom spoke of it, it was too sore a subject; but his attention to the lame bird had from that day to this never relaxed for an instant.

On the way to the village, Sir Everard questioned him on his progress with his lessons.

Humphrey always gave a capital account of himself; reading, writing, French, everything, according to him, was going on as swimmingly as possible.

Sir Everard's faith in these reports had been rather shaken since the memorable occasion when, relying on Humphrey's confident assertion, that he now knew the auxiliary verbs perfectly, he had, with a father's pride, called upon him suddenly to repeat the verb "avoir" to his grandmother. She was a lady of the old school, and a great stickler for early education: and he had been rather nettled by an observation that had dropped from her, to the effect that Humphrey was rather backward.

"Indeed, mother," he had answered, "I think few boys of his age know so much of French. He speaks it perfectly, and is well grounded in the grammar."

To prove which, Humphrey had been called out of the garden, and, to his father's dismay, had conjugated the first tense of the verb in the following manner:—

J'ai
Tu
Il   as
                                                a
Nous   *sommes*
Vous   *étes*
Ils sont.

Conversation did not flag for a moment as they walked along.

On the subject of history, Humphrey not only professed to be, but was, well informed. It gave food to his imagination, and he delighted in it. Sir Everard felt quite brushed up in the early parts of history before they reached the village, and Humphrey himself was so taken up with his subject, that he readily agreed to give up his expedition to the shop, so that they might extend their walk by returning home another way.

"We shall pass little lame Tom, anyhow," he said, "and I can give my pennies to him instead."

Lame Tom was a little cripple, who sat all day long in a little wooden chair, and was an object of great commiseration to Humphrey. A creature who had never known what it was to walk, run, or climb, and had to sit still in a chair from year's end to year's end! How keenly such a condition appealed to the pity of such a nature as Humphrey's!

He gave him his pennies as he passed, and then resumed his conversation with his father.

It was nearly dinner-time when they reached home, and Miles was eagerly waiting for his game of "Spelicans" with Sir Everard. He was, however, never quite happy unless Humphrey was included in his amusements, if he happened to be present: so after a time "Spelicans" was changed to "Old Maid," a game of which both boys were particularly fond.

No "lady of a certain age" could have shown more eagerness to get rid of the fatal Queen than did the two little brothers, and they played as if their whole future depended upon it.

Great was their delight and exultation when, at the end of the game, they found they had both escaped the fate of single blessedness; and, with great clapping of hands and other demonstrations of triumph, Sir Everard was informed that he "would be an old maid."

CHAPTER XII.

It was a lovely day, real harvest weather, when Sir Everard Duncombe and his two little boys took their way to the corn-field to see the new machine at work.

Sir Everard was going up to town that evening, but it was for the last time; and then, to the children's delight, he had promised to come down for good, and had settled that the Harvest Home should take place early in the ensuing week.

The corn-field presented a gay appearance when they reached it. The new machine, drawn by two fine horses, and driven by the bailiff, was careering along the corn, with the reapers all running by the side. Down fell the golden grain on all sides, and eager hands collected and bound it up.

With a shout of joy, Humphrey was among them, hindering every one and alarming his father by continually getting in the way of the machine and the horses.

Of course he was not long content with so subordinate a part in the proceedings; and came to beg his father to let him mount up on the little seat by the bailiff's side.

Sir Everard assisted him up, and the machine went off again, followed by the reapers.

By and by, Sir Everard looked at his watch, and found it was time to be making his way to the station. The children were so happy, he had not the heart to take them away.

"They are quite safe," he reflected, "with so many people about; and I will send Virginie to them, as I pass the house."

Humphrey was out of sight, so Sir Everard told Miles (who was playing with the "little girl at the lodge") to look out for Virginie, and to say "good-bye" for him to Humphrey.

Little Miles held up his face to be kissed—a thin face it was still—and said: "You'll come back soon, Fardie, and not go away any more?"

"Very soon, my darling; and then not leave you again till next year! We'll have great fun, and you must be a good little man, and not get ill any more."

"I promise, Fardie."

Sir Everard smiled rather sadly, kissed the child over and over again, and then walked away.

When he got to the gate, he turned round to have one more look at the gay scene. Miles was still standing where he had left him, gazing after his father, and kissing his hand. His was the prominent figure in the foreground, surrounded by the golden corn. Away behind him stretched the lovely landscape, and in the background was the machine returning to its starting point followed by the reapers. Humphrey, sitting by the bailiff, had now got the reins in his own hands, and was cheering on the horses as he came.

So Sir Everard left them.

Excitement cannot last for ever, and after a time, Humphrey got tired of driving, and got down to play with his little brother. They followed the machine once or twice, picking up the corn, but it was hot work, and they went to rest under the hedge.

"It is very hot, even here," said Humphrey, taking off his hat, and fanning himself. "I think we'll go and sit under the tree in the next field, where we sat the Sunday Uncle Charlie was here. Come along."

They climbed over the gate, and made for the tree, where they sat down on the grass.

"How jolly Uncle Charlie's stories were," sighed Humphrey; "how I wish we could hear them all over again. It's a great pity father ever told me not to climb the bough that sticks out. It would have been the very thing to crawl along, like the man in that story.

109

Father says its rotten and unsafe. I think he *must* make a mistake; it looks as strong as possible!"

He sighed again, and there was a long pause.

Presently he resumed. "I don't see why we shouldn't go and *look*. It would be so cool by the pond."

"Oh! Humphie, *please* don't. We shall lose our way, and Virginie will be so angry."

"But I know the way quite well from here, Miles. It was only because we started from Dyson's cottage that I lost it before."

"But, Humphie, if we get wet again! I *promised* Fardie not to get ill."

"The rain made you wet, Miles, not the pond; and it's not going to rain to-day. Look what a blue sky!"

The two little brothers gazed upwards. It was clear overhead, but there was a suspicious bank of clouds in the distance.

"Those clouds won't come down till night," Humphrey observed. "Come along. It's not very far."

"Better not, Humphie."

"I'm only going to look, Miles. What are you afraid of?"

"Don't know, Humphie," answered the little fellow, with a tiny shake in his voice; "but *please* don't let us go!"

"Well, you needn't come if you don't like. I'll go alone—I shan't be long."

But Miles didn't like being left in the field by himself; so with a little sigh, he got up, and put his hand in his brother's.

"I'll come," he said, resignedly.

"That's right," said Humphrey; "there's nothing to be afraid of—*is* there?"

"No," said the child; but his face was troubled, and his voice still shook a little.

So over the grass the two little brothers went, hand in hand, till in an adjoining field they saw the waters of the pond gleaming like silver in the summer sunshine. Side by side they stood on its brink.

"We're only going to *look*, you know," said Humphrey.

They were the first words he had spoken for some time, and they came so suddenly that Miles started as they fell on the still air. They seemed to arouse the inhabitants of that secluded spot, for a bird flew out of the tree, and soared away with a scared chirrup, which fell with a melancholy sound on the children's ears; and a water-rat bounded from under a lily-leaf, and plunged with a dull splash into another part of the pond.

Innumerable insects skimmed across the surface of the water, and one or two bees droned idly, as they flew from one water lily to another.

The branch of the tree that stretched over the pond dipped its topmost leaves into the water with a sleepy sound; as the breeze swayed it gently backwards and forwards, the water-lilies danced lightly with the movement of the water; and there was over the whole place a sense of repose and an isolation which infected the children with its dreaminess, keeping even Humphrey silent, and making little Miles feel sad.

"Let's go, Humphie."

"Not yet," answered Humphrey, recovering from his fit of abstraction, and moving towards the tree: "I want to look at the branch. Why, it's not rotten a bit!" he exclaimed, as he examined it. "I do believe it would hold us quite well!"

He clasped his arms round the trunk of the tree, and propelled himself upwards, where he was soon lost to view in the thick foliage.

Miles gave a little sigh; he could not shake off the melancholy that oppressed him, and he was longing to get away from the place.

Presently Humphrey's ringing laugh was heard, and Miles, looking up, saw him crawling along the branch which stretched out over the water. His face was flushed, and his eyes sparkling with excitement, and he was utterly regardless of the shivering and shaking of the branch under his weight. When he had got out a certain distance he returned, and throwing his arms once more round the upper part of the trunk, he raised himself to his feet and stood upright, triumphant.

"There!" he exclaimed—"I've done it. Who says it's dangerous now? It's as safe as safe can be. Come up, Miles. You can't think how jolly it is!"

Miles drew a long breath. "Must I really *really* come?"

"Why not? you see how easily I did it. Give me your hand, and I'll help you up."

Bright and beautiful was the aspect of the elder boy, as he stood above, with his graceful figure clearly defined against the green foliage, one arm thrown carelessly round a bough, and the other outstretched to his little brother; and very lovely the expression of wistful uncertainty on the face of the younger one, as he stood below, with his eyes upraised so timidly to his brother's face, and his hands nervously clasped together.

Involuntarily he shrank back a little, and there was a pause.

He looked all around the secluded spot, as if to find help, as if to discover a loophole whereby he might escape, even at the eleventh hour. But the insects skimming from side to side of the pond, the water-lilies dancing gently on the surface, were still the only animate things to be seen, and no sound was to be heard save the dipping of the branch into the water, and the splash of the active water-rat. They were powerless to help him, and he resigned himself to Humphrey's will.

"I know I shall be *kilt*, but I'll come," he said; and he held out his shaking little hand.

Humphrey grasped it tightly, and got him up by degrees to the same level as himself. Then carefully he dropped down on his hands and knees and helped Miles to do the same.

Slowly they both began to move, and gradually they crawled along the branch that stretched over the water! Clinging tightly with arms and legs, and listening to Humphrey's encouraging voice, little Miles settled himself on the branch in fancied security.

Humphrey got close up to him behind, and put his arms round him. "Hurrah" he shouted; "here we both are!"

They had been so engrossed that they had not noticed how the weather had clouded over. The bank of clouds they had noticed was nearly over their heads, the air was becoming thick and oppressive, far in the distance was heard the growl of approaching thunder, and some big drops of rain fell.

Humphrey remembered, with a start, his father's injunctions about Miles, and the ill effects of their last adventure. "We must go home," he exclaimed; and, forgetting their perilous position, he moved so suddenly, that he nearly sent his little brother off the branch. Instinctively he reached out his hand to save him, and Miles nearly overbalanced himself in his attempt to cling to it.

Their combined movements were too much for the decaying wood, already rocking beneath their weight. It swayed—it shivered—it creaked ... and then with a crash it broke from its parent bark!—and boys and branch were precipitated into the water below.

PART II.

PART II.

CHAPTER XIII.

Sir Everard Duncombe pursued his way to the stables on leaving the harvest field; and as he passed the house, he called out to Virginie, who was sitting at work at the nursery window, to go and join the children.

On arriving in London, he went to his club for his letters, and, meeting a friend on the steps, they walked down Piccadilly together, and turned into the park at Hyde Park Corner.

They stood by the railings for a little while, watching the stream of carriages and their gaily dressed occupants; but it was very hot, and after a time Sir Everard took leave of his friend, and strolled towards the Serpentine, in search of a little air.

Miles's delicacy, ever the subject rising uppermost in his mind, occupied his thoughts as he walked along. He wondered to himself whether he would outgrow it, whether a winter abroad would set him up, and whether it would not be wise to bring him to London, and show him to one of the great chest doctors.

The sight of the water, as he approached the Serpentine, recalled to his mind the pond at Wareham, and the expedition which had been the cause of the mischief. He remembered, with a start, how near he had left the children to the tempting spot, for the pond was almost within sight of the field where they were reaping.

For a moment he debated whether he had been wise to trust Humphrey again; but then he reflected how soon Virginie must have joined them, and how many people there were about.

Besides, they were quite taken up with the reaping, and when he remembered his own severe words to Humphrey, and the boy's penitence and remorse, he could hardly fancy he would transgress again.

Still, he could not get it out of his head, and as he stood watching the water, he wished there were such a thing as the magic glass he had read to the children about; that he might see as far as Wareham, and satisfy himself about them.

Had his wish been gratified at that moment, he would have seen Humphrey and Miles astride on the rotten bough, with flushed and exultant faces.

The same change of weather now took place as was taking place at Wareham. Umbrellas and carriage-hoods were quickly put up, and very soon the park was empty.

Sir Everard retraced his steps to his club and was closing his umbrella leisurely in the hall, when a telegram was put into his hand.

He glanced his eye hastily over it, and then dashed into the street and hailed a hansom.

"Waterloo Station," he shouted, as he threw himself into it; "double fare if you catch the train!"

Bustle and confusion, though no doubt, uninteresting and unpoetical, are, certainly, at such times useful. They keep the mind from dwelling too much on the painful, and thus rub off the sharp edge of the first moment.

So it was not till Sir Everard was in the train, and tearing swiftly, though quietly to Wareham, that he realized his position.

Till then, his thoughts had been entirely taken up with passing this carriage, shaving that omnibus, or rounding that corner. He had chafed at every stoppage, fumed at every delay, and been able to think of nothing but whether or no he should catch the train.

And now, the strain over, he leant back in the railway carriage and examined the telegram at leisure.

There was not much to be learnt from it; it was terse and unsatisfactory, like most messages of the kind—just sufficiently clear not to quell all hope, and yet undefined enough to give reins to the imagination. It contained these words: "An accident has happened. Both the young gentlemen have fallen into the pond, but neither are drowned. Come directly."

Those who have read and re-read such missives, and vainly endeavored to extract something from them, will best understand how Sir Everard tortured himself during the next quarter of an hour. Might not this be a part of the truth, and the rest concealed? Might it not be meant as a preparation?

But, no—unless the message told a deliberate falsehood, "neither were drowned." Why, then, bid him come directly, unless Miles's condition after his immersion in the water was all but hopeless. "A ducking will not hurt Humphrey," he reflected "so of course, it is Mile."

He thought of Miles's fragile appearance as he stood in the corn-field. How little he was fitted to cope with such an accident! Fragile and flushed, with traces of his late illness lingering about his lustrous eyes and colorless lips.

He worked himself up into a terrible state of anxiety as the train neared Wareham, and restlessly he laid the blame of the accident on everything and everybody.

What business had they at the pond? he angrily questioned; it was the most flagrant act of disobedience on Humphrey's part he had ever heard of.

For the moment, he felt as if he could never forgive the boy for such a barefaced breach of his command. Over and over again had Miles's health, life even, been endangered by Humphrey's heedlessness.

Heedlessness!—willfulness he felt inclined to call it. Perhaps he was too indulgent. Stricter measures should be enforced; the boy must and should learn to obey. He had been weak, but he would be so no longer. No punishment could be severe enough for Humphrey; and punished he should certainly be.

Then he thought perhaps it was too much to expect of such a young creature and he began to lay the blame on others. Virginie—why was *she* not there? Why did not *she* prevent their going to the pond?

Even the reapers and the bailiff came in for a share of his anger. Surely, among so many people, *somebody* might have prevented two children leaving the field!

But, after all, Humphrey was the chief offender, and he felt he ought not to try to shield him, by throwing the blame on others.

There was no carriage waiting for him at the station, and no one could give him any information beyond that contained in the telegram.

He ordered a fly, and then, unable to bear the delay, walked on without it. He got more and more anxious as he neared the Abbey. He took a short cut to the house. There was no one about—not a servant, not a gardener. His heart misgave him as he strode on. He reached the hall door, passed in, ran up the stairs to the nursery. Still no sound—no voices. The nurseries were empty! He called. No answer. He shouted. How horrible his voice sounded in the empty passages! He rang the bell furiously, and, without waiting the answer, he ran down-stairs again, and opened the library door.

A confused hum of voices struck upon his ear, a confused group of people swam before his eyes, but he only distinguished a little form that ran forward with outstretched arms; and with an exclamation of fervent thanksgiving he clasped Miles safe, warm, and unhurt in his arms!

How eagerly he felt the little pulse and chafed the little hands! He stopped the child's mouth with kisses whenever he attempted to speak.

He was so occupied with his newly recovered treasure, that he did not notice what a deep silence had fallen on the assembled group on his entrance; but now he turned to one of the maids, and asked how the accident had happened. "And, by the way," he added, "where is Master Humphrey?"

No one answered.

"Where is Master Humphrey?" repeated the baronet.

"They told me not to say," began little Miles; but his father was looking directly at one of the gardeners, and the man was obliged to answer.

"If you please, Sir Everard, we carried Master Duncombe in there," pointing to the drawing-room.

"In *there!*" said the baronet, amazed.

"If you please, Sir Everard, it was the first room we came to; and the only one where there was a sofa."

Before he had done speaking, Sir Everard was in the room. A shutter had been opened, and there was just light enough for him to see Virginie bending over the sofa, round which was a group of people.

The doctor came forward from among them, but Sir Everard pushed past him, and advanced to the side of the sofa.

And there, under his mother's picture, colorless, motionless, and to all appearance lifeless, lay the boy for whom "no punishment could be severe enough," and whose disobedience he had felt he never could forgive!

CHAPTER XIV.

No one was to blame. The reapers had run to the pond on hearing the children's cries, and had extricated them immediately; Virginie had sent for the doctor at once. So no one had failed in their duty; or had, as I say, been to blame—except the poor little victim himself.

"At present," the doctor informed Sir Everard, "the extent of the injuries could not be determined."

Miles, from having been jerked off the end of the branch straight into the water, had escaped with a wetting; but Humphrey, from having been nearer the tree, had come in contact with the trunk, and the bough under the water, and the doctor feared both spine and head had been injured. He asked for further advice, and a man was dispatched with a telegram for two of the greatest surgeons of the day.

The calamity was so sudden, so awful, so unexpected! Sir Everard could not realize it—kept on misunderstanding the doctor's incoherence—the poor old doctor who had known him all his life, and could not bear to be the one to tell him that, even if his boy's life were spared, he must ever be a helpless cripple.

Humphrey a cripple! Humphrey to lie on his back all his life! Sir Everard could not grasp the idea, could not collect his thoughts to conceive anything so impossible, could not follow the doctor through the circumlocution in which he tried to clothe the announcement, and at last lost patience.

"For God's sake, tell me what you mean! Can you be trying to break to me that my boy—that child who has never to my knowledge sat still in his life—will never have the use of his limbs any more? Speak out, I implore you!"

"Never any more, Sir Everard!—never any more."

*   *   *   *   *   *   *   *   *

Still he could not realize it, could not take it in.

He turned away, and went out into the air, to clear, as it were, the mistiness of his brain, and to bring himself face to face with the words, so as to *force* himself to understand them. "Never have the use of his limbs any more!" Simple English words—he knew he must really understand them, and yet they seemed to him mere sounds, devoid of any signification.

He repeated them over and over again, to see what he could make of them. "Never have the use of his limbs any more." That meant—let him think it out clearly—it meant, that his boy, his restless, impetuous boy, would be chained to a sofa all his life, for ever cut off from all that glorified his young existence—*that* was what it meant. It meant—for now that thought was beginning to assert herself, each word that was meaningless before, was becoming alive with signification—it meant that all that had been should be again no more—that all that the child called *life* was over—that all that went to make up the sum of his existence was gone—that death in life must be his portion for ever and for ever!

For what did the word *life* mean to Humphrey? Why, the powers of which he was to be deprived were the very germs of his whole existence—the things for which he was, and moved, and had his being. Take them away, and what remained? Life bereft of these, what was it to him? What is a husk from which the kernel has been taken, or a casket from which the jewel is gone?

Sir Everard was not a worldly man, and in those moments he did not dwell on the blighted youth, and blasted manhood; he did not think of the earthly career for ever clouded, the hopes of earthly distinction for ever shut out. He did not see that his boy was debarred from every path of usefulness or honor which man delights to tread—alike shut out from active service, and learned profession. Results painful enough in themselves; but it is none of them that have brought that despairing expression to his set, white face. No!

He is thinking of the active little figure, chained to an invalid's chair. He is trying to realize that the lawns and gardens will know

121

his joyous presence no more. Surrounded by the haunts of the young life, he is forcing himself to believe that all henceforth shall be lone and silent, that never again shall they echo to his light footstep, or ring with his merry laugh; that the active limbs shall be motionless, and the busy hands for ever still. And only one word rose to his lips, "Impossible!"

At moments like these, how our feelings are reflected on all things around. Never before had Sir Everard so keenly realized the endless motion of nature.

With the probable fate of his boy lying before him, he was perhaps exaggerating the blessing of movement; but certainly he had never before so forcibly noticed how every little leaf on the trees fluttered as the breeze passed over it, how every little blade of grass shook and danced in the wind, how the boughs swayed and the blossoms nodded, how the waters of the streamlet rippled and leapt on their way!

And this with what is called *inanimate* nature; and when it came to the birds, and the beasts, and the insects!

It was cruel of two lambs to come and gambol together at that moment, just under the poor father's eyes; cruel of a little rabbit to choose that second, out of all the hours of a long summer day, to pop up from under the brushwood, and scamper away across the green grass! When had the air ever been so full of butterflies, horseflies, and beetles; for ever and ever on the wing! The bees hurried from flower to flower, the birds chased each other from tree to tree, the summer gnats never rested for a moment;—and Humphrey, of all Nature's children the happiest and the brightest, was to be the one who should sport in the sunshine no more!

He thought of the boy's restless activity, his joy in motion and exercise. From dawn to sunset, never still, never weary of rushing about in the open air. There had always been with him a sort of lavish enjoyment of existence for its own sake, as if there were happiness in the mere sense of *being* and *moving*.

Even as a little baby it had always been the same. When he could scarcely stand alone, he would struggle to get out of his nurse's arms, and start off by himself, heedless of the many falls he would get on the way. And as memory brought back the early days of the child's life, came mingled with them the thought of the mother who had so delighted in him. And as Sir Everard remembered how she had gloried in his manly spirit, and in his energy and activity, he bowed his head, and thanked God that she had not lived to see this day.

Once more he saw her restraining her maternal fears that she might not interfere with her boy's love of enterprise, or bring a shadow on his happiness. Once more he seemed to hear the baby voice at the bed-room door, before the shutters were opened.

"Mother, mother, may I go out?"

The breathless pause till the answer came.

"Out now! My darling, it is so early and so cold. Better wait a little!"

"The insides of houses are so hot, mother; please say I may go out!" ...

Had the boy ever walked? Had he ever done anything but run?

Sir Everard could not recall one instance of meeting him out of doors, except running and rushing headlong, jumping over everything which obstructed his path.

Once again, there rose the thought of the motionless little figure sitting pale and silent in a cripple's chair. God help the poor father! In the bitterness of his spirit he had almost said, "Sooner than clip his wings, let him soar away."

He retraced his steps, and on entering the hall, was informed by the trembling Virginie that Humphrey had recovered consciousness, and had spoken.

He hurried to the drawing-room, but the doctor met him at the door, and motioned him back.

"Do not go in just yet," he said, closing the door behind him; "he seems to fear your displeasure about something, and shows great excitement at the thought of seeing you. I dare say," he added, quickly, for he was touched by the expression of pain which passed over the poor father's face, "I dare say he will get over it, when he is a little less confused."

"Does he understand what has happened?"

"I think so, now. At first he was sadly confused at finding himself in the drawing-room; but by degrees he remembered the events of the day. The moment he grasped the idea of the accident, he became excited, and asked repeatedly for his little brother. I should fancy this anxiety was associated with his shrinking from seeing you. Perhaps you understand better than I do?"

"I have been obliged several times lately to find fault with him for leading his little brother into mischief, and this last unfortunate escapade I had most especially forbidden. Miles is, as you know, so very delicate that I am obliged to be very careful of him."

This was said almost in an exculpatory tone.

"He is certainly very delicate," answered the doctor, "and ought not to be exposed to such dangers. I am very thankful he has escaped so easily. Now my little patient's constitution is altogether different; seldom have I seen a finer or stronger. However," he added, breaking off with a sigh, "the most iron frame is not proof against such an accident as this. I think, Sir Everard," he concluded, "that what you tell me would quite account for the excitement. May I tell him from you that he has no cause to fear your anger?"

"Need you ask?" said the baronet, impatiently, and the doctor returned to the sick room.

Sir Everard paced up and down till the door re-opened, and the doctor made him a sign to come in.

He entered, and advanced to the side of the sofa. The room was so dark that he could only see the outline of the curly head, lying back among the pillows, but a little hand came out, and pulled him down.

"Father," in a voice which was hardly above a whisper, "it's all right. He isn't hurt a bit—not even a cold. I am so glad it is me that is hurt instead of him."

"Oh, hush! hush! my darling."

"You're not angry with me, father? I'm so sorry I climbed. I'll never do it again. Say you're not angry, father."

"No, no my poor child—I'm not angry only so sorry to see you ill."

"Am I *very* ill? What is the matter with my head? Shall I soon be well again?"

"I hope so, darling. There are some gentlemen coming to-morrow, to help you to get well very quick."

"I shall be well by the Harvest Home shan't I?"

"The Harvest Home? When is that?"

"You promised to fix a day early next week, you know, father. Which day shall it be?"

"I—I don't—quite know what day to fix, my boy."

"The corn fell so fast, all day, father—it must be ready soon. Shall we say Tuesday?"

No answer: only an inarticulate murmur.

"Then that's settled. Shall I be well enough on Tuesday to dance 'Up the middle and down again,' with Dolly?"

Rises again, all unbidden, before the father's eyes, a motionless little figure, sitting in a cripple's chair. Dance! Ought he to tell him? ought he to prepare him? who was to do it, if not he? who else was to tell him of the blight that had fallen on his young life?

"You don't tell me, father. Shall I be well soon?"

He *could* not tell him. He only kissed the little hand, and murmured, "God grant you may, my child!"

"I shan't be able to lie still very long. If it wasn't that I feel so tired, I should like to jump up now."

"Are you very tired, Humphrey?"

"Yes," with a sigh, "and my back aches, and so does my head, and feels so funny. It makes my eyes swim, and that makes me so sleepy."

"Will you try to go to sleep?"

"Yes," murmured the child, and his heavy eyes closed; "I shall wake up quite well to-morrow."

"A good sign," whispered Sir Everard to the doctor. The doctor did not answer; and Sir Everard went up to the nursery, to see Miles. The little fellow was gazing out of the window, humming a forlorn little tune to himself. Jane, with red eyes, was sitting at work.

Sir Everard took the child up in his arms "What are you doing, my little man?"

"I'm so dull without Humphie. When will he come and play?"

"Soon, I hope, darling."

"Is Humphie going to sleep all night in the drawing-room?"

"Yes—isn't that funny?"

"May I go and say good-night to him?"

"No; you can't go to him to-night."

Miles's eyes filled with tears. "I can't go to sleep without saying good-night to Humphie."

"Ah! don't cry, my child," said the poor father, beseechingly. His feelings had been on the strain so many hours; he felt he could not stand any more, and he dared not let his thoughts dwell on the

126

subject. He tried to turn the conversation. "Tell me," he said, with a forced smile, "what was that little song you were singing to yourself when I came in?"

"It was about Humpty-Dumpty," said Miles, mournfully.

"Let me see: Humpty-Dumpty, was an egg, wasn't he?"

"That gentleman said it was Humphie who was Humpty-Dumpty. Is that true, Fardie?"

"No, darling; how could Humphrey be an egg?"

"One part's true, though," said Miles, "'Humpty-Dumpty had a great fall.'"

"Ah! that's true!" sighed Sir Everard.

"What's the end, Fardie? I want to remember it, and I can't—do you?"

Why did Sir Everard put the child down so suddenly, and why should his voice falter a little, as he repeated the baby couplet? They were only nursery rhymes, and this is how they ended:

"All the king's horses, and all the king's men,
Will never set Humpty-Dumpty up again."

"It's 'diculous nonsense, Fardie, of *course*?"

"A ridiculous nonsensical rhyme, darling!"

But ah! how nearly the sublime and the ridiculous touch sometimes in this world!

CHAPTER XV.

Humphrey passed the night partly in heavy sleep and partly in feverish restlessness.

His first inquiry in the morning was for Miles, and the next for the gentlemen who were to help him to get well so quick.

The latter he was told could not arrive till eleven o'clock, but Sir Everard went to fetch little Miles, and whispering to him not to talk much or to stay long, he put the child down and stayed by the door to watch the meeting between the two little brothers.

Miles advanced rather timidly, the room was so dark and everything looked so strange. But as soon as he distinguished his brother he ran forward.

"Humphie! get up, get up. Why do you 'ie there, and look so white?"

"I'm ill, Miles!"—in a tone half plaintive, half triumphant.

"*Musn't* be ill, Humphie—oh, don't be ill!"

"*You're* often ill, Miles; why shouldn't I be ill sometimes?"

"Don't like it," said the child, his eyes filling with tears. "Oh, Humphie, I wish we hadn't *tummelled* into the pond!"

At this moment Sir Everard was called away, and informed that the physicians had arrived from London.

He found them in the dining-room, talking over the case with the village doctor and, after ordering them some breakfast, he returned to prepare the little invalid for their arrival.

As he approached the room he was alarmed to hear Humphrey's voice raised, and still more, when little Miles, with a face of terror came running out.

"Oh, Fardie, Fardie! will you come to Humphie? He's crying so, and he wants you to come directly!"

"Crying so! What is the matter with him?"

"Oh, I don't know? He began to cry and scream so when I said it!"

"Said what—said what?"

"Oh, Fardie, I was telling him that I heard Virginie tell some one he would be 'boiteux' all his life, and I *only* asked him what it meant!"

*　　*　　*　　*　　*

Vainly all night long had Sir Everard tried to frame a sentence in which to convey the fatal news.

Phrase after phrase had he rejected, because nothing seemed to him to express half the love and tenderness in which so terrible an announcement should be clothed. Words were so hard, so cold! They were so weak to express what he wanted—so utterly inadequate to contain all the pity, all the yearning sympathy with which his heart was overflowing!

And now without any preparation, without any softening, the cruel blow had fallen!

For one moment the father's heart failed him, and he felt he *could* not face the boy, *could* not meet his questioning gaze, *could* not with his own lips confirm the fatal truth. But there was no time for reflection. Humphrey's feeble voice calling him to come quickly, caught his ear, and as in a dream he advanced, and stood by the bedside.

"Father!" exclaimed the child (and how shall we express the tones of his voice, or convey an idea of the pitiful entreaty and nameless horror with which they rang?) "it isn't true—is it? Oh, say it isn't true!"

All the words of consolation and soothing died upon the father's lips, and his tongue seemed tied.

"She's always saying unkind things," sobbed the child, clinging to him; "she oughtn't to—*ought* she? You don't answer me, father! Father, why don't you tell me? Why don't you say quick, it's not true?" And as his fear grew, his voice faltered, and his grasp on his father tightened. "Answer me—father—why—don't you—speak?"

"My poor child, my poor little fellow!" One more struggle for the truth, in spite of the failing voice, and the sense of deadly sickness.

"Lift up your face, father. Let—me—see—your—face!"

What was there in the face that struck terror to his heart, and brought conviction thumping up in great throbs, even before the faltering words came.

"Supposing it should be true—what then!"

Ah! what then? His dizzy brain refused to attach any meaning to the words, or to help him to understand how much was contained in them.

The loud beating of his heart echoed them, his parched lips strove to repeat them, and wildly he fought with his failing senses, straining every nerve to find an answer to the question. In vain! Every pulse in his throbbing head seemed to take up the words and beat them into his brain; the air was live with voices around him, and voices and pulses alike cried, "What then?—what then?" But the question went unanswered, for Humphrey fainted away.

*　　*　　*　　*　　*

Sir Everard hastily summoned the doctors, and they did all they could to restore him.

In a little while he showed signs of coming to himself, and to prevent his thoughts returning to the subject which had agitated him, they requested Sir Everard to remain out of sight, and stationed themselves close to the bedside, so that theirs should be the first figures that should attract his attention.

As Humphrey slowly recovered consciousness, he did not indeed clearly remember on what his thoughts had been dwelling, but that there was something in his mind from which he shrank, he was quite aware.

Waking in the morning to a sense of some sorrow which possessed us ere we slept, we intuitively feel there is something amiss, though we are too confused to remember what it is; and even while we wish to recall it, we dread to turn our thoughts that way, lest we should lose the temporary peace into which forgetfulness has plunged us.

In such a passive state would Humphrey have remained, had not the doctors, to distract his thoughts, touched his brow, and caused him to open his eyes.

Alas! they little knew the all-powerful association of the place where he lay.

He closed his eyes again directly, and took no notice of the doctors' attempts to lead him into conversation; but in that one moment, his glance had rested on his mother's picture, and at once his mind wandered back—not indeed to the memory they dreaded, but to one which was scarcely less painful.

We will follow his thoughts for a moment.

He is alone; all alone in the desolate apartment, in the closed uninhabited room! The twilight is creeping slowly on, and the silence and emptiness within and without him, can almost be felt. Up-stairs in the nursery, Miles is dying—perhaps already dead. No one will help him, or be sorry for him. And as the sense of neglect and isolation steals over him once more, his breast heaves, and his lips move:

"Mother, I want you back so much, every one is angry with me and I am so very miserable!"

No answer, no sound.

"Mother! put your arms round me! put my head on your shoulder!"

Not a word.

It is only a picture after all.

*   *   *   *   *

Never to play with Miles any more! No more games on the stairs,
or in the passages! No, never more! For Miles is dying, perhaps
already dead. How happy the baby in the picture looks! Can it
really be him? Oh, happy baby, always close to mother! always
with her arms round him, and her shoulder against his head. Oh, if
he could climb up into the baby's place, and stay there for ever
and ever! How *could* he get up to her? She is in Heaven. She got
there by being ill and dying. Why should he not get ill, and die
too. Miles is dying, mother is dead—he would so like to die too.
But it's no use. He never is ill—not even a cold. Miles caught cold
going to the pond—the pond where the water-lilies are. How quiet
it was! how cool! How gently they dance upon the water, those
lovely water-lilies. How the bird sang, and the rat splashed....
Come up, Miles—it's as safe as safe can be!... Stop!... Miles is
dying—how could he come up? Miles came into the room, and
talked about the—jackdaw ... wasn't it?—the poor lame
jackdaw.... Miles is dying.... How did he come in?... Hop! hop!
comes the jackdaw, poor old fellow! But what did Miles say about
the jackdaw? Boiteux! But *that's* not his name; we always call him
Jack. Boiteux means.... The jackdaw again! Hop, hop, he comes....
He will never fly again—never! Poor old jackdaw!... Is it ready
true that he will never fly again? It is not true. But supposing it
should be true, what then?... Boiteux!... Who is it keeps on asking
me what 'boiteux' means?... Boiteux! "What then?" Boiteux means
jackdaw—no, it means lame—no it means crip——

The temporary oblivion is over, the unknown dread is taking a
tangible shape, and recollection rushes over him, bringing
conviction with it.

But Hope, ever the last gift in the casket, faintly holds out against
certainty.

"No! no!—not that! it *can't* be that!"

132

But something beating in his heart, beats Hope down. Mighty throbs, like the strokes of a hammer, beat it down, down, crush it to nothing; and a terrible sinking comes in its place. *It is true—* and in an instant he realizes what *It* being true will entail.

As lightning, flashing upon the path of the benighted traveller, reveals to him for a moment the country lying before him, illumining all its minutest details; so thought, flashing upon the future of the child, showed him for a moment all too vividly the life of crippled helplessness stretching out before him—the daily, hourly cross, which must be his for ever!

Let each one try to conceive for himself the intensity of such a moment, to such a nature!

Let each one try to realise the thoughts which followed each other in hot haste through his brain, the confused phantasmagoria which swam before him, fading away at last, and leaving only two distinct pictures—the jackdaw hopping about in his cage, and little lame Tom in the village, sitting in his cripple's chair.

He shrinks back in horror, his soul rises in loathing: he pants, and wildly throws himself about, with a half-smothered cry.

"Oh, gently, my darling! you will hurt yourself."

It is his father's voice, and he turns to him and clings tightly.

"I don't care—I don't care. I want to hurt myself. I want to die. I don't want to live like that!" At the sight of the physicians, his excitement redoubled, and he clung more tightly to his father. "No! No! Send them away! They shan't look at me, they shan't touch me. They are going to try and make me well, and I don't want to get well. I *won't* get well!"

The doctors retired, as their presence excited him so much, and Sir Everard tried to loosen the boy's convulsive grasp round his neck.

Humphrey was too exhausted to retain the position long: his hands relaxed their hold, and Sir Everard laid him back on the pillow.

Once more the soft face in the picture exercises its old influence over him, and charms away, as of old, the fit of passionate rebellion.

"Father," he entreated, in a whisper, "let me die! Promise not to let them try and make me well again."

Between surprise and emotion Sir Everard could not answer. He thought the idea of death would be both strange and repugnant to so thoughtless a creature; and he marvelled to hear him speak of it.

"You'll promise, won't you, father? You know I *couldn't* live like that! Let me go and live with mother in Heaven. See," pointing to the picture, "how happy I was in her arms when I was a baby, and I want to lie there again so much! Just now, when I thought it was still the night Miles was ill, before I knew I should never walk or run any more, even then I wanted so to get ill and die, that I might go to her, and I want it more than ever now. I thought then I never could get ill, because I am so strong; but now I *am* ill, and so you'll let me die! Promise not to try and make me well?"

Three times Sir Everard strove to answer, and three times his voice failed him. He managed, however, to murmur something which sounded like an affirmative, which satisfied and quieted the child.

But much of the boy's speech had been wholly unintelligible to him, and his allusions to his mother's picture especially puzzled him. Looking upon the drawing-room as a closed room, he had no idea that the children ever penetrated into it, or that they knew of the existence of the picture. And laying his hand on the child's head, he said: "How did you know that was your mother, Humphrey?"

The boy shot at him a glance of such astonishment that Sir Everard felt rebuked, and did not like to continue the conversation; and the doctors, returning at that moment, it was not resumed.

This time, Humphrey made no resistance, and the physicians were able to make their examination.

Leaving the village doctor by the bedside, Sir Everard led the way to the library, to hear their opinion.

He hardly knew what he wished. Humphrey's horror at his impending fate had made such an impression on Sir Everard that he almost shrank from hearing the child would recover to such a life as that. And yet when the doctors told him his boy must die, a revulsion of feeling swept over him, and his rebellious heart cried, "Anything but that!"

"Would it be soon?" he tried to ask.

"It could not be far off," they said.

"Would the child suffer?"

"They hoped not—they believed not;" and they wrung his hand and departed.

He followed them to the hall door, and waited with them till their carriage came up.

It was a still summer's morning when they came out upon the steps, as if all nature were silently and breathlessly awaiting the verdict. But as the doctors got into their carriage, a light breeze sprang up, causing the trees to sway and rustle with a mournful sound, as if they knew the sentence, and were conveying it to the fields around. Sir Everard stood watching them as they drove away—those great court physicians, who, with all their fame and all their learning could do nothing for his boy—nothing!

He listened to the sighing of the wind, and watched the trees bowing mournfully before it; and he wondered vaguely what was the language of the winds and breezes, and in what words nature was learning his boy's fate. It seemed to him that the breezes pursued the retreating doctors, and flung clouds of dust around them, as if taunting them with their inability to help; and then, returning once more to the oaks and beeches, resumed their melancholy wail. Dreamily there recurred to his mind that ancient fable the children loved to hear: that story of the olden time which tells how the wind wafted through the trees to the passers-by, the secret which had been whispered into the bosom of the earth:

"List! Mother Earth; while no man hears,
King Midas has got asses' ears."

And, as he cast one more look at the carriage in the distance, before re-entering the house, the messages of the breezes seemed to come into his head in the form of the baby rhymes he had so often heard the children sing.

CHAPTER XVI.

Before returning to the sick-room, Sir Everard sat down to write some letters.

He tried to think of some one he could send for, to help him in his trouble. His mother was too infirm to leave home, his sister perfectly useless, and they were the only relations he had.

His brother-in-law was the person who would have been the greatest comfort to him, but he had just been appointed to a ship, and Sir Everard knew him to be up to his neck in preparations, perpetually veering between London and Portsmouth. As, however, he must pass Wareham Station on his journeys to and fro, Sir Everard wrote to beg him if possible, to stop for one night on his way.

Then he went up to the nursery. Miles was having his mid-day sleep; and Jane, the housemaid, was sitting by his crib. Sir Everard bent down to kiss the little fellow, who was lying with his face hidden, hugging to his breast some ears of dead corn; but as his father's lips touched his forehead, he stirred in his sleep, and said, "Humphie."

"What has he got there?" asked Sir Everard of Jane.

"Some ears of corn, I think, Sir Everard," answered Jane; "it's some that belonged to Master Humphrey, and he says no one shan't touch it but himself. I heard him say he had found it in a corner of the nursery, and that Master Humphrey must have put it there, and forgotten it, for that he had meant to plant it in his garden."

Sir Everard did not answer: he stooped over the little sleeper, and kissed him again tenderly. "Whatever you do, don't wake him," he whispered; "let him sleep as long as ever he can."

He left the room; and as he went down-stairs the children's conversation in the cornfield that Sunday afternoon recurred to him, and he could not help making a mental comparison between the young corn and the young life, both so suddenly uprooted from the earth.

Meeting the doctor in the hall, he briefly communicated the physicians' opinion, and begged him to make it known to the household. To announce it himself, he felt to be impossible.

He found the worn-out child in a heavy sleep when he reached the drawing-room; there was nothing to draw his thoughts from the subject upon which they had been dwelling, and he found himself going over and over the scene in the corn-field. He seemed to see and hear it all with startling distinctness. Wherever he looked, he saw Humphrey sitting on the top of the gate with the ears of corn in his destroying hand and Miles looking sorrowfully up at him.

He could not bear it at last, and walked up and down the room, to get it out of his head. But even then their voices rang in his ears, and filled him with pain.

"Never mind, Miles," sounded in clear bell-like tones the voice which would never rise above a whisper again. "I will plant them in the sunny bit of our own garden, where the soil is much better than here, and where they will grow much finer than if they had been left to ripen with the rest. Perhaps they will thank me some day for having pulled them out of the rough field, and planted them in such a much more beautiful place."

But he might have found comfort instead of pain in the words, had he followed out the metaphor which had been floating in his head. For would not the child one day thank Death, the destroyer; who in uprooting him fresh and green from the earth, would transplant him to the rich soil of God's own garden; where, in the sunshine of His Maker's presence, he should ripen into that perfection, which is unknown among the children of men?

For natures like Humphrey's are not fit for this rough world. Such a capacity for sorrow has no rest here, and such a capability for enjoyment is fittest to find its happiness in those all-perfect pleasures which are at God's right hand for evermore.

*   *   *   *   *   *   *   *   *

139

Humphrey was seldom conscious during the days that followed. He was either in heavy sleep, or incoherent rambling.

He would lie talking to his mother's picture in a whisper; going over games and conversations with Miles; or wandering on unintelligibly to himself.

Whenever he was aware of his father's presence, he would complain of a curious noise in his head, and ask what the rushing and singing in his ears meant; but before he got an answer, he would ramble off again, and take no notice of what was passing around him.

Sir Everard, sitting for hours by his bedside, often thought of the boy's allusions to his mother's picture, and of the look with which Humphrey had greeted his inquiry as to how he had known it was she.

Many words that at times dropped from the child, puzzled him, and he often longed to question him on the subject.

Seeing one night a gleam of consciousness in the dark eyes, he went closer to the sofa, and tried to attract the boy's attention.

"What are you thinking about, Humphrey?"

"Mother," he answered, in a faint voice; "when is she coming to fetch me?"

But before there was time for an answer, he was overcome by his usual drowsiness, and Sir Everard's opportunity was gone. But perhaps what bewildered him most was the way in which the child had prayed to be allowed to die.

To Sir Everard, with his one-sided view of the boy, it was all such an enigma.

Here was a child who had always seemed so entirely taken up with the pleasures of the passing moment, that his past and future were alike merged in the enjoyment of the present—a creature on whom sorrow and loss had produced no permanent impression passing over him, as it were, only to leave him more gay, more heedless than ever. *Permanent* impression! why, as far as Sir Everard knew, they had produced no impression at all!

Five days after his mother's death, he had seen him romping and playing as usual, and from that day to this, her name had never passed his lips! And *now* he talked of her as if her memory were very fresh and familiar; and looked upon death as calmly as if he had been contemplating it all his life.

What did it mean? When had he thought upon such things? How was it that he, who had enjoyed to the full the pleasures of his young life, should be so ready to renounce them all?

Sir Everard was fairly baffled, as he asked himself the question over and over again.

Is it, then, so difficult to understand? Sir Everard should have gone to Wordsworth, and learnt his lesson there.

"Children," he says, "are blest and powerful:—

> "Their world lies more justly balanced,
> *Partly at their feet, and part far from them."*

This is the answer to the question. A child lives, no doubt, in his surroundings throws himself heart and soul into the pleasures or the sorrows of the moment; and is immersed in the interests of the path which lies straight before him.

But this is not all. Talk to any child for a few minutes, and see, if, in the description of his hopes and joys some such phrases as these do not occur: "When I get big;" "When I am a man;" "Some day when I am older."

He is looking for something else; he is reaching on to some state he knows not of, but which is to be more perfect than his present one.

> "Sweetest melodies are those
> That are by distance made more sweet"

141

There is something else waiting for him—worlds not realized—glories as yet unknown. In what will consist their charm, he knows not; but the vague is the possible, and the unknown is the glorious. So, perhaps, the "Land which is very far off" is more present to him than it is to those of riper years; not so much more shadowy than any other part of the transcendent future lying before him.

A child's world is so full of mystery too. Everything is so wonderful and unexplained, that the "Things unseen and eternal" are scarcely more incomprehensible than the things unseen and temporal. Where everything is so strange, one thing is not much more strange than another.

Look how many inexplicable things are occurring every day around him. Take the mysteries of birth and death, for instance. How soon he grows familiar with them. In a few days, the new little brother or sister seems as though it had always been there; and when the loss does not occur *in* the house, or affect him very nearly, he seldom asks questions after the rush that follows the first announcement, but contents himself with a general résumé of the occurrence in some such a train of thought as this: "Poor mamma was crying yesterday; and we are all going to have black frocks."

He takes everything upon trust, believing implicitly everything which is told him: he never cavils or argues, or reasons. He believes his elders infallible—in fact, he must: have they not proved right over and over again? Not being able to understand, he *must* trust; and to a boundless faith and a vivid imagination *all* things are possible!

*   *   *   *   *

It may be that some such ideas as these did at last float across the mind of Sir Everard, as he sat by the boy, who from first to last had been misunderstood.

One day Humphrey woke with a start, as if from a dream, and said eagerly: "Didn't you promise they shouldn't make me well?"

"Yes, my darling."

"I thought for a moment—or I dreamt—that I was getting well—and—it was——"

"It was what?" asked Sir Everard, trembling lest a wish for life should be springing up in the boy's breast, and that the regrets, whose non-existence he had marvelled at, should be going to overpower him at last.

"It was so horrible!" said the boy.

Strange that we should be subject to such sudden revulsions of feeling! The very words which set the father's mind at rest, jarred upon his feelings, and before he was aware, he had said, almost reproachfully, "Horrible, Humphrey! to stay with me?"

"You forget, father—you forget what I should be."

"But I would have made it so happy for you, my little Humphrey," burst from Sir Everard. "You should never——"

He stopped, for there was a far-away look in the boy's eyes, and he was gazing intently at the picture.

Sir Everard thought he was not listening. But in a few minutes he spoke.

"I am thinking I should not have minded it so much, if mother were here. I could lie in her arms all day, like I used then (pointing to the picture); but now——"

"You could lie in my arms, my darling."

"In *yours*, father? you've always got Miles. You never take *me* in your arms."

"I didn't ever think you would care to come, my little Humphrey."

"Oh! but I often should though; only I knew you would rather have him."

"Oh! hush! hush! When have you wanted to come?"

"Well, not so *very* often, father—only sometimes—a good while ago."

"But, my child, I would just as soon have had you as Miles. I only take him because he is so small. Why do you say I would rather have him?"

"I thought so, father, because you smiled quite differently when you looked at him, and called him your darling much more than you did me, and kissed him—oh! so much oftener."

Sir Everard could have implored the child to stop. He took the thin hand in his and caressed it.

"Miles is such a baby you know. I did not think you would be jealous of him."

"Jealous?" said Humphrey, rather puzzled; "jealous means angry—doesn't it?"

"Well—yes; I suppose it does."

"Oh, then, I wasn't jealous," said the boy, earnestly, "because I never was angry. Poor little Miles couldn't remember mother, you see, and I could—so it was quite fair. Only now and then— sometimes it——"

"What, dear boy?"

"It made me want mother so *dreadfully*," said Humphrey, his eyes filling with tears. "But now," he added, dreamily, for the drowsiness was beginning to overpower him, again, "I'm going to her, or at least God's going to send her to fetch me." And he closed his heavy eyes.

Sir Everard sat on, meditating. He mused on the by-gone time when his wife had told him Humphrey was as loving as Miles and he had inwardly denied it; he mused on the responsibility of bringing up children, and the necessity of living constantly with them to hope to understand the complications of their characters; and sadly he reflected on the irreparable loss his children had sustained in the mother, who would have done it all so well.

He was not a morbid man, and he did not reproach himself for what had been unavoidable; for a man belongs more to the world than to his home; and his home ought not to throw any hindrance in his path of usefulness. But he told himself plainly that he had failed; that, satisfied if his children were well and happy, he had been content to go no further, and to remain in ignorance of all that Humphrey's simple words had disclosed.

He was filled with admiration for the generous nature which had borne so patiently to see another preferred, and had charmed away the feeling which *had* arisen sometimes, by the reflection, "It is quite fair."

He thought how the same circumstances acting upon a different temperament might have produced jealousy, discontent, and bitter feeling; the little brothers might have grown up to hate each other, and he would never have perceived it. And with an uncontrollable feeling he knelt down by the bedside, and covered the child with kisses.

Humphrey opened his eyes and smiled. "I was dreaming of mother," he said; "she was asking me if you had sent her any message."

"Tell her, my darling, how much I love you, and how sorry I am to let you go."

"So sorry to let me go," he repeated, with the old expression of triumph coming into his face; "and that you love me very much; as much as Miles, shall I say."

"As much as Miles," said Sir Everard.

"And that's quite true, father?"

"Quite true, my own precious child."

A smile flitted over his face, and he shut his eyes, saying, "I've often forgotten your messages before, father, but I shan't forget this one!"

*   *   *   *   *

145

Presently he roused up again, and said, "I should like to do that thing people do before they die."

"What thing?"

"I forget the name of it in English. In French it is the same as the Gospels and Epistles."

"The same as the Gospels and Epistles? What can you mean?"

"Virginie calls them 'Le Noveau Testament.' What's the English for that?"

"New Testament."

"But what's testament in English? I can't remember words now."

"Testament in English? Oh! will."

"Oh, yes!—will—that's it. Well, I want to make my will; will you write it down as I say it?"

Sir Everard fetched some writing materials, and drew a little table to the bedside.

Humphrey dictated. "In large letters first, father, write—

"HUMPHREY'S WILL

"I leave my knife with the two blades to Miles. One of the blades is broken, but the other is quite good, and Virginie needn't be afraid of his hurting himself, because it has been quite blunt and rusty ever since I cut Carlo's nails with it, and left it out all night in the rain. And Dolly must take care of my garden, and not let the flowers die. And father, you're to have my prayer-book and my microscope; and I suppose I must leave Virginie my little gold pin, because she's asked me for it so often, and I shall never grow up now to be a man, and wear it with a blue scarf, like I always meant to. And Dolly may have one of my books. I don't think she would understand 'Peter Parley,' so perhaps it had better be the 'Boy Hunters.' Then there's the ferret, and the guinea-pigs, and the rabbits. I think Dolly shall have them too, because I know she'll take care of them. What else have I got? Oh, yes! there's my fishing-rod, and my skates, and my cricket things, all those are for Miles. I've got twopence somewhere; I don't exactly know where, but give them to lame Tom in the village; and tell him I'm more sorry for him than ever now. And will somebody be kind to my poor jackdaw? I know you all think him very ugly, and he *is* cross, and he *does* peck, but please, for my sake, take care of him, because I'm the only friend he has in the world, and now I'm going to leave him. Perhaps lame Tom had better have him, because he'll understand better than any of you, how sad it is to be—lame—and obliged to be still in one place all day. My little sweet-pea in the nursery window is for Jane. It takes a great deal of water. I used to pump my whole little pump of water on it four or five times a day. It never was strong, that little sweet-pea. Sometimes I think it had *too* much water. But Jane will settle that.

"Well! I think that's all. Good-bye everybody."

"Have you put 'Good-bye everybody?'" he asked, eagerly.

"Yes," answered Sir Everard, vainly endeavoring to steady his voice, "I have put it, dear. Is there anything more?"

"Don't people write their names, father? Could I write mine, do you think, myself?"

"I don't think so, my darling," his father returned, in the same husky tone; "but I will write them for you."

"All of them, please, father—Humphrey, and Everard, and Charles. Isn't it a lot!" exclaimed Humphrey, with a touch of his old merriment.

"There it is in full," said Sir Everard; "Humphrey Everard Charles Duncombe."

"May I try and make a mark, father?"

"If you like, dear," said the father, sadly; for he knew it was impossible that the poor little hand and arm should perform such an office, and Humphrey saw it himself directly he tried to move, and abandoned the attempt of his own accord.

"Now hide it away somewhere, father," he exclaimed, eagerly, "for no one must read it yet. I'm glad I've made my will," he added, as, with a sigh of weariness, for he was worn out by so much talking, he closed his eyes, and disposed himself to sleep.

Half-an-hour after, a letter was put into Sir Everard's hand. It was from his brother-in-law, and contained these few lines:

> "MY DEAR EVERARD,—I have a few days to spare, and will come down to Wareham on my way to Portsmouth. Tell Humphrey I hope to be in time for his Harvest Home, and beg him to find me a pretty partner.
>
> "Yours, etc."

Sir Everard turned the letter over to look at the date. It could not surely be the answer to his letter! But on examining the post-mark, he found that it had been written some days previously from Portsmouth, and that it was directed to his club in London, from whence it had been forwarded.

"He has never got mine," he reflected, "Poor fellow! what a shock it will be when he arrives."

At that very moment Uncle Charlie was reading Sir Everard's letter at an hotel in London. It dropped from his hand, and he remained wrapped in sad meditation.

"Too late to-night," he said at last, looking at his watch, "but by the first train to-morrow morning."

He roused himself, and went to the window. There, looking down upon the ceaseless stream of carriages in the busy street below, his thoughts reverted to the Sunday at Wareham, and the boy's strength and beauty. He thought of him as he had last seen him, radiant with health and spirits, waving his hat on the door-step as the dog-cart drove away. But perhaps recollection brought the child most clearly before him creeping up his leg, when he came to say "Good-night," and begging for more stories on the morrow.

"Going to-morrow! what a short visit!"

"I will pay you a longer visit next time."

"But when will next time be?"

"Yes, when will next time be?"

*   *   *   *   *   *   *   *

"Ah! when indeed?" sighed Uncle Charlie.

CHAPTER XVII.

Brightly rose the week which had been fixed for the Harvest Home, but it was welcomed by no festivities in the fields and meadows of Wareham Abbey.

The flags and tents which had been prepared were stored away again; the holiday dresses were put by unfinished; Dolly, the laundry-maid, hid away, with a great sob, the flaming yellow print with a red spot she had been all the way to the market town to buy; and village mothers, standing in groups at their cottage doors, whispered together with tearful eyes, and made faint attempts to keep their own restless boys in sight.

There was mourning far and wide for the young life that was passing away, and rough voices faltered as they spoke of the bright face and ringing laugh which should be known no more among them.

Humphrey was sinking rapidly; but like a lamp which, before it goes finally out, flickers into something like a bright flame, did his brain, after those many days of wandering unconsciousness, seem to regain something of its wonted vigor.

"What does it mean?" he asked his father over and over again, whenever he opened his eyes.

"What does what mean, my darling?"

"Why, this funny noise here"—touching his head.

"It means that your poor head aches."

"Oh! but it means something else; it's a sort of rushing and singing noise, always rushing and singing. What is it like? Do help me to remember!"

Sir Everard racked his brain to satisfy the poor little questioner, but to no purpose.

"You're not trying, father," said the little fellow peevishly.

150

Sir Everard wondered to himself whether the child could be thinking of the rushing of water in the ears described by people rescued from drowning, and answered—

"Is it like the sound of water?"

"Yes, yes!" exclaimed Humphrey; "it's like the sound——," he stopped, and then added, "of many waters."

He seemed struck by his own words.

"What is that, father? Where have I heard that? What is it like?"

Sir Everard thought he had satisfied him, and was distressed to hear the question again, fearing he would exhaust himself by so much talk.

"I told you before, darling, it is like a sound of water."

"That's all wrong," he said, mournfully, half crying, "it's not *water*, it's *waters*—many waters."

"Yes, yes, my child," said Sir Everard soothingly, alarmed at his agitation.

"But say it again, father; say it right through."

Sir Everard repeated, "A sound of many waters."

"There!" exclaimed Humphrey, "*now* what is it? You must know what it means now!"

Sir Everard was more puzzled than ever, having thought that they had come to an end of the discussion.

"I *really* don't know, my boy!"

"If *you'd* got a sound of many waters in your head, father, you'd like to hear what it means! Oh, where did I hear all about it? Where have I been? Who was near me? You were there, father, I know, for I remember your face; and all the while somebody was telling us what the rushing and singing in my head means!"

Sir Everard thought the boy was wandering, and did not try to answer him any more. He was accustomed to sit for hours by the bedside, while Humphrey rambled incoherently on. It was no use trying to follow the poor little brain through the mazes of thought into which it now plunged.

Presently Humphrey startled him by saying—

"What does Charlie mean?"

"Well, nothing particular, darling."

"But it does, it does," said the child. "Does it mean the same thing as a sound of many waters?"

"Yes, yes," said his father, still thinking he was wandering.

"Then if I say 'a sound of Charlie,'" said Humphrey, "it means the same as 'a sound of rushing and singing in my head?'"

"No, no, dear," answered Sir Everard, surprised to find him so rational.

"Why, you said 'Yes,' just now," said the child, with a sob. "If you tell stories, father, you'll go to hell like.... *Who* was it told stories about the wild men's dinner party?" he concluded, excitedly.

"Uncle Charlie," answered his father, "but he didn't tell stories, dear, it was only a joke."

He turned his head away as he spoke, for the mention of the dinner-party brought up the image of the boy bursting into the library full of life and health and beauty, and the contrast with the little worn-out figure lying on the bed overcame him for a moment.

But the latter part of the speech, and his father's emotion, were lost upon Humphrey and he only repeated to himself over and over again, "Uncle Charlie, Uncle Charlie. Is that what I mean? What is Uncle Charlie? Who is Uncle Charlie?"

At this moment there is a sound as of an arrival; voices and footsteps outside; but Humphrey hears them not. Some one knocks at the library door. One of the maids in the distance steals gently towards it, for Sir Everard holds up his hand to enforce silence, hoping that the busy brain may get a few moments' rest. The door opens, and a young man enters. Sir Everard rises, and goes to meet him. After a few moments' whispered conversation, both advance noiselessly to the sofa, and stand looking at the little face on the pillow with its closed eyes. Closed, but not sleeping. The weary brain is trying to rake up, from its fragmentary recollections of the past, something that may throw a light on his present perplexities. Dim, confused figures flit across the stage of his fancy, glimmer, and disappear.

"Stop!" he cries feebly, as if the moving shadows wearied his brain; "oh, please stand still!"

Roused by the sound of his own voice, he opens his eyes, and, ere he closes them again, fixes them for a moment on the form standing by his bedside. Hush! do not break the spell! The mists are clearing, the shadows becoming more distinct. From the fleeting chaos before him one figure now stands out more clear, more immovable than the rest—the figure of a tall, fair man. Hush! he has found the clue! The grey walls of the old church are rising around him; the sides of the old pew are towering above him. Just in front of him is the large prayer-book, surmounted by the monogram "Adelaide," and by his side the tall, fair man! Hush it is all coming back now.

In the distance sits his father, with his legs crossed, and his head turned towards the pulpit, where stands the old clergyman, with his Bible in his hand. Breathlessly the boy listens for the words he longs to hear; but no sound comes from the lips of the preacher. Disappointment comes down upon his spirit, when, in his vision, the figure sitting by him takes out a pencil, and underlines something in his Bible.

"Of course," cries Humphrey out loud, "he knows; he can tell me. Uncle Charlie!" The real figure by the bedside starts and comes forward, but Sir Everard holds him back.

"He is only dreaming, don't disturb him."

"It *was* Uncle Charlie," murmurs Humphrey; "and he can tell me. Many waters and a pencil and a Bible ... and Uncle Charlie sitting there ... and then ... there came in his face...."

To the consternation of the by-standers, Humphrey went off into fits of weak laughter. The association of ideas recalled another circumstance; his mind has wandered away from the point on which it was fixed, and he is watching again the encounter between his uncle and the wasp.

"He'll be stung!" he cries, shaking with laughter, and he puts his wasted hand to his mouth, as if he knew he was in church, and ought to check himself. The figure by the bedside turns to Sir Everard, and whispers, but the only answer is—

"Nothing but a dream. For God's sake do not awake him."

Thoroughly exhausted, Humphrey is lying still again, but now his mind is once more perturbed, for his uncle's figure has disappeared from his vision, and he tries to conjure it before him in vain.

"He is gone!" he exclaims, with a sob, "just as I was going to ask him. Oh, come back, come back, Uncle Charlie!"

Some one kneels by his side, some one lays a hand on his brow and he opens his eyes with a start. The church, the pew, the prayer-book—all are gone—but in their place—his uncle!

"Oh, Uncle Charlie!" sobbed the child, trying to throw his feeble arms round his neck, "is it really you? Where do you come from? *You'll* tell me all about it; *you'll* help me to remember!"

"Tell you what, my dear, dear little fellow?"

"I don't know what! I can't tell what! It's something I want to remember, and I don't know what it is!"

"What was it like?" asked Uncle Charlie.

"It was like a church," answered Humphrey, excitedly, "and it was like a summer's morning, and you and me and Father sitting still, while somebody was telling us what the sound in my head means. I *can't* remember what he said, but if I *only* could I shouldn't mind the rushing and singing a bit; for when I heard it that time, everything about it was happy, and bright, and beautiful. But you were there, Uncle Charlie, and you must know, for you wrote something down about it."

"I told you so, Everard," said the young man to his brother-in-law; "I knew he was trying to remember the sermon on the Revelations we heard the Sunday I was down here."

"But you're not telling me, Uncle Charlie," sobbed Humphrey.

"I will, my boy, I will; but you must let me go and fetch my Bible, for I don't remember the words exactly."

"Must you go?" faintly uttered Humphrey. "Oh, don't go, Uncle Charlie; you'll disappear like you did just now, and perhaps never come back again."

Uncle Charlie reassured him, and gently disengaged himself from his grasp.

"Be quick! be quick!" panted the child, and his voice failed him with his excitement. Sir Everard tried to soothe him, and hoped he would be quiet. But a few minutes after his uncle was gone, it became evident that Humphrey was struggling to say something before his uncle should return. His excitement and exhaustion made him more incoherent than usual, and after once or twice repeating his uncle's name, his voice failed altogether, and though his white lips moved, no sound came.

Sir Everard was greatly distressed; the boy fixed his eye so pleadingly on him, he was so earnest in what he was trying to say, that it went to the father's heart not to be able to understand him. He strained every nerve to catch the words, but in vain.

The excitement of hearing his uncle returning gave Humphrey a momentary strength, and he held his father's hand with all the strength he could muster, and said, "Promise!"

"I promise, my darling," said Sir Everard, hastily, too thankful to catch even a word.

And nobody ever knew that the boy's last request had been that never, never was his uncle to know that it was his story that had first made him think of the branch that stretched over the pond where the water-lilies grew.

Quite worn out he allowed himself to be laid back upon his pillow, and with closed eyes waited while his uncle opened the Bible and found the underlined passage:—

"And I heard a voice from heaven as the voice of many waters ... and I heard the harpers harping with their harps. And they sang as it were a new song ... and no man could learn that song, but the hundred and forty and four thousand which were redeemed from the earth."

*   *   *   *   *   *

No more restless questions, no more perplexed search after what is lying somewhere in the past. He did not speak, he did not answer his father's eager enquiry as to whether that was what he had been trying to remember; and he lay so still, so motionless, that for one moment they thought he had passed away without hearing the words he had longed for. But the unsatisfied look had gone from his face, and his father saw that his mind was at rest. He was breathing gently as in a deep sleep.

That is all the watchers saw. And the child himself! How shall we attempt to follow the hazy imaginings of his weak and wandering mind?

Dreamily are returning to him the thoughts which had possession of him that summer Sunday as he sat in his corner in the old grey church. Visions of beauty are floating before him, evoked that day in his mind by the powerful imagery of Scripture; now recalled by association: the material joys which form a child's idea of heaven—the gates, and the harps, and the angels. Dim conceptions of white-robed thousands wandering in the golden Jerusalem, by the jasper sea. Not strange to him that throng of angels, for foremost among them all, more beautiful than any, is the figure of his mother, standing as in the picture, looking down upon him with a smile. Heaven to him is peopled with her image, for he has no other notion of all that is fair and holy. In that great multitude whom no man can number, there is not one that can be called a stranger, all have the soft eyes and the familiar smile.

What recks he more of the throbbing and singing in his aching head—the sounds as of rushing waters? Is it not all explained? It is the voice of many waters and the voice of the great multitude, singing the wondrous song which only they can sing! The preacher heard it that Sunday morning; did he not say, "I heard a voice from heaven"? and Humphrey hears it now! Imperfectly as yet it sounds upon his ear, faintly the echoes are borne to him, but it will sound more clearly soon!

It was not in vain that the old clergyman had warmed and glowed with his subject, and by the very earnestness of his own feeling carried his little hearer with him; for his words, though they had lain dormant during the weeks which followed, apparently wasted and forgotten, were, by the power of association, rising when they were needed to bless and soothe his death-bed.

Faint is the heart of the preacher, oftentimes, as he watches his congregation disperse; for he fears that his words, even though they chained the minds of his hearers for the moment, will pass away as they pass the threshold, and be lost in the worldly interests which meet them at the very door.

And yet it may be, that all unknown to him, perhaps in the very hearts he would least have expected, his words have taken root, and will bear fruit some day.

Deep silence reigned in the room, while the two men watched the child.

It was very long before he spoke again, but when he did, it was evident that he was not himself.

"It is getting very dark," he murmured, and Sir Everard's heart sank within him, for the sun was only just beginning to set. "It is time for us to go to bed. Where's Miles?"

For a few brief moments the throbbing has ceased, and with its cessation, voices and visions have fled away.

Sir Everard stole away to fetch the little fellow, and found him in his nightgown repeating his evening prayer to Virginie. With a few hasty explanations, Sir Everard took him in his arms, and carried him away.

"But, Fardie," said Miles, as they hurried downstairs "I hadn't quite finished; I have not said my hymn."

"Never mind, darling! you shall say it to Humphrey to-night."

He carried him gently into the drawing room, and set him down upon the sofa.

Miles was frightened at the silence and darkness, and nestled up closer to his brother.

"Humphie! Humphie! wake up and give me your hand."

"Don't be frightened, Miles," murmured Humphrey, dreamily: "come close to me, I'll take care of you."

He strove to move to the edge of the sofa, as if he thought his little brother's bed was close up against it, and he threw his feeble arm round Miles in the dear old protecting way.

"We won't talk much to-night, Miles, because I'm so very sleepy. Good-night."

He said something faintly about seeing his mother, but Miles couldn't catch the words.

"Didn't quite understand, Humphie."

Something of a movement of impatience passed over Humphrey's face.

"Of course you don't—because—you can't—remember her."

"No," said little Miles, meekly, "but you'll tell me, Humphie?"

"To-morrow," he murmured, "I shall be able to explain—better—to-morrow—good-night—good-night."

And in the silence that reigned, every one present heard the little brothers exchange their last kiss.

  * * * * * * * *

"I can't see them," said Sir Everard, huskily; "some one draw up the blind."

The setting sun outside was illumining the landscape ere it sank to rest, and shedding its beams on the haunts and the companions of the boy's young life. On the lambs he had chased in the meadows, on the birds he had watched since they had learned to fly, on the fields and the gardens which seemed so empty without him, it was shining with a softened glow;—but it seemed to have reserved its richest glory for the children, for, as the blind went slowly up, such a flood of light poured into the room, that the eyes of the father were dazzled, and it was some minutes before he could distinguish them.

There, in the golden sunset, they lay. The sun kissed their little faces, and touched with a loving hand their curly hair. It lingered lovingly round them, as if it knew that the lambs would be frisking when it rose again, the birds would welcome it with their glad song; but that never again would it rest on the nestling forms and clasped hands of the two little brothers!

Sir Everard, bending over them, saw a troubled expression over Humphrey's face.

"What can it be that ails the child?" he mentally questioned; "is it physical pain, or is something troubling his thoughts? Is the fear of death coming over him?"

He did not like to speak for fear of disturbing him, but as the look deepened almost to pain, he could not restrain himself any longer.

159

"Humphrey, my darling," he exclaimed, in his longing to do something, be it ever so little, to soothe his boy's dying hour, "what is it? What can I do for you?"

Nothing! With all his love and all his yearning, nothing!

For surging once more in the boy's brain is the noise as of rushing and singing, and with its sound a fear has risen in his breast. Shall he ever, ever catch the music of that wondrous song? Doubts of his own power to learn it are troubling his wandering thoughts; dim misgivings that *children* can not learn it, founded on his own inability to follow the singing in church. Always too soon or too late! *Do* children ever learn it? "'And no *man* could learn that song save the hundred and forty and four ...' nothing about children *there*!"

Vain is the father's endeavor to reach a trouble of this kind; vainly, bending over him, does he seek to discover its cause, in his longings to remove or alleviate it.

Is the child, then, to pass away uneasy, with a cloud upon his happiness; or must a miracle be worked in his favor? Must Heaven open and show him the army of innocents standing at the right hand of God? No. God's ways are not as our ways: infinite in power, He yet reveals Himself by the simplest means.

As once before He sent the child consolation so will He send it now. As once before, not by signs and wonders, but by the gift of sleep, so now, not by miracles and visions, but by the voice of his baby brother.

"Talk to me, Humphie. Don't go to sleep yet. I haven't said my hymn. Fardie said I might say it to you to-night. Shall I say it now?"

Without waiting for an answer, Miles raised himself on his knees, and put his little hands together. Then arose the sound of the baby voice:

160

"Around the throne of God in Heaven
　　Thousands of children stand;
Children whose sins are all forgiven,
　　A holy, happy band.
　　　　Singing Glory, Glory, Glory."

*　　*　　*　　*　　*

Faster and louder comes the rushing and singing, but the misgiving is lulled to rest. Faster and faster, louder and louder, surging around him. But hushed are the doubts at once and for ever, and the fear has vanished away! Loud in his brain sounds the song of the children, throbbing there almost to pain; beating so loud as to stun and confuse him. Everything seems to be turning and whirling; and, as if to save himself, he opens his eyes. On what a sight did they fall! There, close before him, bathed in light, and a glory round her brow stands the figure of his mother, looking down upon him with a smile. And with a glad smile of welcome he stretched out his arms, and cried, "Has God sent you to fetch me at last, mother? Oh, mother, I'll come! I'll come!"

*　　*　　*　　*　　*

Those who were standing round, saw only the expression of pain change to the old sunny smile. His lips moved, and he lifted his arms, as his eyes were raised for a moment, to the picture above him, on which the sun was pouring a dazzling light. They closed; but the smile, intensely radiant, lingered about the parted lips; the short breathing grew shorter ... stopped ... and then....

"It's no use my saying the rest," said little Miles in a whisper, "for Humphie has gone to sleep."

Finis.

End of the Project Gutenberg EBook of
Misunderstood, by Florence Montgomery

*** END OF THIS PROJECT GUTENBERG EBOOK
MISUNDERSTOOD ***

***** This file should be named 55222-h.htm or
55222-h.zip *****
This and all associated files of various formats
will be found in:
        http://www.gutenberg.org/5/5/2/2/55222/

Produced by MWS, Martin Pettit and the Online
Distributed
Proofreading Team at http://www.pgdp.net (This
file was
produced from images generously made available
by The
Internet Archive/American Libraries.)

Updated editions will replace the previous one--
the old editions will
be renamed.

Creating the works from print editions not
protected by U.S. copyright
law means that no one owns a United States
copyright in these works,
so the Foundation (and you!) can copy and
distribute it in the United
States without permission and without paying
copyright
royalties. Special rules, set forth in the
General Terms of Use part
of this license, apply to copying and
distributing Project
Gutenberg-tm electronic works to protect the
PROJECT GUTENBERG-tm
concept and trademark. Project Gutenberg is a
registered trademark,
and may not be used if you charge for the
eBooks, unless you receive

specific permission. If you do not charge
anything for copies of this
eBook, complying with the rules is very easy.
You may use this eBook
for nearly any purpose such as creation of
derivative works, reports,
performances and research. They may be modified
and printed and given
away--you may do practically ANYTHING in the
United States with eBooks
not protected by U.S. copyright law.
Redistribution is subject to the
trademark license, especially commercial
redistribution.

START: FULL LICENSE

THE FULL PROJECT GUTENBERG LICENSE
PLEASE READ THIS BEFORE YOU DISTRIBUTE OR USE
THIS WORK

To protect the Project Gutenberg-tm mission of
promoting the free
distribution of electronic works, by using or
distributing this work
(or any other work associated in any way with
the phrase "Project
Gutenberg"), you agree to comply with all the
terms of the Full
Project Gutenberg-tm License available with this
file or online at
www.gutenberg.org/license.

Section 1. General Terms of Use and
Redistributing Project
Gutenberg-tm electronic works

1.A. By reading or using any part of this
Project Gutenberg-tm
electronic work, you indicate that you have
read, understand, agree to
and accept all the terms of this license and
intellectual property

(trademark/copyright) agreement. If you do not agree to abide by all
the terms of this agreement, you must cease using and return or
destroy all copies of Project Gutenberg-tm electronic works in your
possession. If you paid a fee for obtaining a copy of or access to a
Project Gutenberg-tm electronic work and you do not agree to be bound
by the terms of this agreement, you may obtain a refund from the
person or entity to whom you paid the fee as set forth in paragraph
1.E.8.

1.B. "Project Gutenberg" is a registered trademark. It may only be
used on or associated in any way with an electronic work by people who
agree to be bound by the terms of this agreement. There are a few
things that you can do with most Project Gutenberg-tm electronic works
even without complying with the full terms of this agreement. See
paragraph 1.C below. There are a lot of things you can do with Project
Gutenberg-tm electronic works if you follow the terms of this
agreement and help preserve free future access to Project Gutenberg-tm
electronic works. See paragraph 1.E below.

1.C. The Project Gutenberg Literary Archive Foundation ("the
Foundation" or PGLAF), owns a compilation copyright in the collection
of Project Gutenberg-tm electronic works. Nearly all the individual
works in the collection are in the public domain in the United
States. If an individual work is unprotected by

copyright law in the
United States and you are located in the United
States, we do not
claim a right to prevent you from copying,
distributing, performing,
displaying or creating derivative works based on
the work as long as
all references to Project Gutenberg are removed.
Of course, we hope
that you will support the Project Gutenberg-tm
mission of promoting
free access to electronic works by freely
sharing Project Gutenberg-tm
works in compliance with the terms of this
agreement for keeping the
Project Gutenberg-tm name associated with the
work. You can easily
comply with the terms of this agreement by
keeping this work in the
same format with its attached full Project
Gutenberg-tm License when
you share it without charge with others.

1.D. The copyright laws of the place where you
are located also govern
what you can do with this work. Copyright laws
in most countries are
in a constant state of change. If you are
outside the United States,
check the laws of your country in addition to
the terms of this
agreement before downloading, copying,
displaying, performing,
distributing or creating derivative works based
on this work or any
other Project Gutenberg-tm work. The Foundation
makes no
representations concerning the copyright status
of any work in any
country outside the United States.

1.E. Unless you have removed all references to
Project Gutenberg:

1.E.1. The following sentence, with active links to, or other
immediate access to, the full Project Gutenberg-tm License must appear
prominently whenever any copy of a Project Gutenberg-tm work (any work
on which the phrase "Project Gutenberg" appears, or with which the
phrase "Project Gutenberg" is associated) is accessed, displayed,
performed, viewed, copied or distributed:

   This eBook is for the use of anyone anywhere in the United States and
   most other parts of the world at no cost and with almost no
   restrictions whatsoever. You may copy it, give it away or re-use it
   under the terms of the Project Gutenberg License included with this
   eBook or online at www.gutenberg.org. If you are not located in the
   United States, you'll have to check the laws of the country where you
   are located before using this ebook.

1.E.2. If an individual Project Gutenberg-tm electronic work is
derived from texts not protected by U.S. copyright law (does not
contain a notice indicating that it is posted with permission of the
copyright holder), the work can be copied and distributed to anyone in
the United States without paying any fees or charges. If you are
redistributing or providing access to a work with the phrase "Project
Gutenberg" associated with or appearing on the work, you must comply
either with the requirements of paragraphs 1.E.1 through 1.E.7 or

166

obtain permission for the use of the work and
the Project Gutenberg-tm
trademark as set forth in paragraphs 1.E.8 or
1.E.9.

1.E.3. If an individual Project Gutenberg-tm
electronic work is posted
with the permission of the copyright holder,
your use and distribution
must comply with both paragraphs 1.E.1 through
1.E.7 and any
additional terms imposed by the copyright
holder. Additional terms
will be linked to the Project Gutenberg-tm
License for all works
posted with the permission of the copyright
holder found at the
beginning of this work.

1.E.4. Do not unlink or detach or remove the
full Project Gutenberg-tm
License terms from this work, or any files
containing a part of this
work or any other work associated with Project
Gutenberg-tm.

1.E.5. Do not copy, display, perform, distribute
or redistribute this
electronic work, or any part of this electronic
work, without
prominently displaying the sentence set forth in
paragraph 1.E.1 with
active links or immediate access to the full
terms of the Project
Gutenberg-tm License.

1.E.6. You may convert to and distribute this
work in any binary,
compressed, marked up, nonproprietary or
proprietary form, including
any word processing or hypertext form. However,
if you provide access
to or distribute copies of a Project Gutenberg-

tm work in a format
other than "Plain Vanilla ASCII" or other format
used in the official
version posted on the official Project
Gutenberg-tm web site
(www.gutenberg.org), you must, at no additional
cost, fee or expense
to the user, provide a copy, a means of
exporting a copy, or a means
of obtaining a copy upon request, of the work in
its original "Plain
Vanilla ASCII" or other form. Any alternate
format must include the
full Project Gutenberg-tm License as specified
in paragraph 1.E.1.

1.E.7. Do not charge a fee for access to,
viewing, displaying,
performing, copying or distributing any Project
Gutenberg-tm works
unless you comply with paragraph 1.E.8 or 1.E.9.

1.E.8. You may charge a reasonable fee for
copies of or providing
access to or distributing Project Gutenberg-tm
electronic works
provided that

* You pay a royalty fee of 20% of the gross
profits you derive from
   the use of Project Gutenberg-tm works
calculated using the method
   you already use to calculate your applicable
taxes. The fee is owed
   to the owner of the Project Gutenberg-tm
trademark, but he has
   agreed to donate royalties under this
paragraph to the Project
   Gutenberg Literary Archive Foundation. Royalty
payments must be paid
   within 60 days following each date on which
you prepare (or are
   legally required to prepare) your periodic tax

returns. Royalty
   payments should be clearly marked as such and sent to the Project
   Gutenberg Literary Archive Foundation at the address specified in
   Section 4, "Information about donations to the Project Gutenberg
   Literary Archive Foundation."

* You provide a full refund of any money paid by a user who notifies
   you in writing (or by e-mail) within 30 days of receipt that s/he
   does not agree to the terms of the full Project Gutenberg-tm
   License. You must require such a user to return or destroy all
   copies of the works possessed in a physical medium and discontinue
   all use of and all access to other copies of Project Gutenberg-tm
   works.

* You provide, in accordance with paragraph 1.F.3, a full refund of
   any money paid for a work or a replacement copy, if a defect in the
   electronic work is discovered and reported to you within 90 days of
   receipt of the work.

* You comply with all other terms of this agreement for free
   distribution of Project Gutenberg-tm works.

1.E.9. If you wish to charge a fee or distribute a Project
Gutenberg-tm electronic work or group of works on different terms than
are set forth in this agreement, you must obtain permission in writing
from both the Project Gutenberg Literary Archive Foundation and The

Project Gutenberg Trademark LLC, the owner of
the Project Gutenberg-tm
trademark. Contact the Foundation as set forth
in Section 3 below.

1.F.

1.F.1. Project Gutenberg volunteers and
employees expend considerable
effort to identify, do copyright research on,
transcribe and proofread
works not protected by U.S. copyright law in
creating the Project
Gutenberg-tm collection. Despite these efforts,
Project Gutenberg-tm
electronic works, and the medium on which they
may be stored, may
contain "Defects," such as, but not limited to,
incomplete, inaccurate
or corrupt data, transcription errors, a
copyright or other
intellectual property infringement, a defective
or damaged disk or
other medium, a computer virus, or computer
codes that damage or
cannot be read by your equipment.

1.F.2. LIMITED WARRANTY, DISCLAIMER OF DAMAGES -
Except for the "Right
of Replacement or Refund" described in paragraph
1.F.3, the Project
Gutenberg Literary Archive Foundation, the owner
of the Project
Gutenberg-tm trademark, and any other party
distributing a Project
Gutenberg-tm electronic work under this
agreement, disclaim all
liability to you for damages, costs and
expenses, including legal
fees. YOU AGREE THAT YOU HAVE NO REMEDIES FOR
NEGLIGENCE, STRICT
LIABILITY, BREACH OF WARRANTY OR BREACH OF
CONTRACT EXCEPT THOSE

PROVIDED IN PARAGRAPH 1.F.3. YOU AGREE THAT THE FOUNDATION, THE
TRADEMARK OWNER, AND ANY DISTRIBUTOR UNDER THIS AGREEMENT WILL NOT BE
LIABLE TO YOU FOR ACTUAL, DIRECT, INDIRECT, CONSEQUENTIAL, PUNITIVE OR
INCIDENTAL DAMAGES EVEN IF YOU GIVE NOTICE OF THE POSSIBILITY OF SUCH
DAMAGE.

1.F.3. LIMITED RIGHT OF REPLACEMENT OR REFUND - If you discover a
defect in this electronic work within 90 days of receiving it, you can
receive a refund of the money (if any) you paid for it by sending a
written explanation to the person you received the work from. If you
received the work on a physical medium, you must return the medium
with your written explanation. The person or entity that provided you
with the defective work may elect to provide a replacement copy in
lieu of a refund. If you received the work electronically, the person
or entity providing it to you may choose to give you a second
opportunity to receive the work electronically in lieu of a refund. If
the second copy is also defective, you may demand a refund in writing
without further opportunities to fix the problem.

1.F.4. Except for the limited right of replacement or refund set forth
in paragraph 1.F.3, this work is provided to you 'AS-IS', WITH NO
OTHER WARRANTIES OF ANY KIND, EXPRESS OR IMPLIED, INCLUDING BUT NOT
LIMITED TO WARRANTIES OF MERCHANTABILITY OR FITNESS FOR ANY PURPOSE.

1.F.5. Some states do not allow disclaimers of certain implied
warranties or the exclusion or limitation of certain types of
damages. If any disclaimer or limitation set forth in this agreement
violates the law of the state applicable to this agreement, the
agreement shall be interpreted to make the maximum disclaimer or
limitation permitted by the applicable state law. The invalidity or
unenforceability of any provision of this agreement shall not void the
remaining provisions.

1.F.6. INDEMNITY - You agree to indemnify and hold the Foundation, the
trademark owner, any agent or employee of the Foundation, anyone
providing copies of Project Gutenberg-tm electronic works in
accordance with this agreement, and any volunteers associated with the
production, promotion and distribution of Project Gutenberg-tm
electronic works, harmless from all liability, costs and expenses,
including legal fees, that arise directly or indirectly from any of
the following which you do or cause to occur: (a) distribution of this
or any Project Gutenberg-tm work, (b) alteration, modification, or
additions or deletions to any Project Gutenberg-tm work, and (c) any
Defect you cause.

Section 2. Information about the Mission of Project Gutenberg-tm

Project Gutenberg-tm is synonymous with the free

172

distribution of
electronic works in formats readable by the
widest variety of
computers including obsolete, old, middle-aged
and new computers. It
exists because of the efforts of hundreds of
volunteers and donations
from people in all walks of life.

Volunteers and financial support to provide
volunteers with the
assistance they need are critical to reaching
Project Gutenberg-tm's
goals and ensuring that the Project Gutenberg-tm
collection will
remain freely available for generations to come.
In 2001, the Project
Gutenberg Literary Archive Foundation was
created to provide a secure
and permanent future for Project Gutenberg-tm
and future
generations. To learn more about the Project
Gutenberg Literary
Archive Foundation and how your efforts and
donations can help, see
Sections 3 and 4 and the Foundation information
page at
www.gutenberg.org

Section 3. Information about the Project
Gutenberg Literary Archive Foundation

The Project Gutenberg Literary Archive
Foundation is a non profit
501(c)(3) educational corporation organized
under the laws of the
state of Mississippi and granted tax exempt
status by the Internal
Revenue Service. The Foundation's EIN or federal
tax identification
number is 64-6221541. Contributions to the

Project Gutenberg Literary
Archive Foundation are tax deductible to the
full extent permitted by
U.S. federal laws and your state's laws.

The Foundation's principal office is in
Fairbanks, Alaska, with the
mailing address: PO Box 750175, Fairbanks, AK
99775, but its
volunteers and employees are scattered
throughout numerous
locations. Its business office is located at 809
North 1500 West, Salt
Lake City, UT 84116, (801) 596-1887. Email
contact links and up to
date contact information can be found at the
Foundation's web site and
official page at www.gutenberg.org/contact

For additional contact information:

    Dr. Gregory B. Newby
    Chief Executive and Director
    gbnewby@pglaf.org

Section 4. Information about Donations to the
Project Gutenberg
Literary Archive Foundation

Project Gutenberg-tm depends upon and cannot
survive without wide
spread public support and donations to carry out
its mission of
increasing the number of public domain and
licensed works that can be
freely distributed in machine readable form
accessible by the widest
array of equipment including outdated equipment.
Many small donations
($1 to $5,000) are particularly important to
maintaining tax exempt
status with the IRS.

The Foundation is committed to complying with the laws regulating
charities and charitable donations in all 50 states of the United
States. Compliance requirements are not uniform and it takes a
considerable effort, much paperwork and many fees to meet and keep up
with these requirements. We do not solicit donations in locations
where we have not received written confirmation of compliance. To SEND
DONATIONS or determine the status of compliance for any particular
state visit www.gutenberg.org/donate

While we cannot and do not solicit contributions from states where we
have not met the solicitation requirements, we know of no prohibition
against accepting unsolicited donations from donors in such states who
approach us with offers to donate.

International donations are gratefully accepted, but we cannot make
any statements concerning tax treatment of donations received from
outside the United States. U.S. laws alone swamp our small staff.

Please check the Project Gutenberg Web pages for current donation
methods and addresses. Donations are accepted in a number of other
ways including checks, online payments and credit card donations. To
donate, please visit: www.gutenberg.org/donate

Section 5. General Information About Project Gutenberg-tm electronic works.

Professor Michael S. Hart was the originator of

175

the Project
Gutenberg-tm concept of a library of electronic works that could be
freely shared with anyone. For forty years, he produced and
distributed Project Gutenberg-tm eBooks with only a loose network of
volunteer support.

Project Gutenberg-tm eBooks are often created from several printed
editions, all of which are confirmed as not protected by copyright in
the U.S. unless a copyright notice is included. Thus, we do not
necessarily keep eBooks in compliance with any particular paper
edition.

Most people start at our Web site which has the main PG search
facility: www.gutenberg.org

This Web site includes information about Project Gutenberg-tm,
including how to make donations to the Project Gutenberg Literary
Archive Foundation, how to help produce our new eBooks, and how to
subscribe to our email newsletter to hear about new eBooks.